HEALING FATE

HEALING FATE
A Westin Pack Novel

By

Julie Trettel

Healing Fate
A Westin Pack Novel: Book Seven

Cover Art by, Bookin' It Designs

Thanks and Acknowledgments

Big thank you to all my readers who originally read this as a novella in the duet Shifter Marked and Claimed and came back to hear more of Micah and Lucy's story. This one's for you!

Lucy

Chapter 1

"Mommy!"

The blood curdling scream cut through the night's air. My heart raced as I shot out of bed and ran down the hall.

Vada was thrashing in her bed still asleep. Night terrors. She'd been battling them ever since our rescue and it slayed me to see her tiny form in such agony.

I picked her up and held her to me. It took some force as she shook and kicked out.

"Shh. Mommy's here. You're okay, Vada. You're safe."

I gently rocked her as I spoke soothing words until her body went still, almost lifeless.

The first time that had happened I had freaked out. I was a complete mess for days afterwards. I knew now it was just part of the process.

My daughter didn't get these terrors every night, but when she did it generally meant a long night coming for the both of us.

I carefully laid her back down on her bed and tucked the covers around her as tears streamed down my face. In the big scheme of things, this had been an easy one. It sometimes took hours to settle her, not minutes. It was sad to say that tonight was a rare treat.

I sat on the floor next to her bed watching and waiting. I was certain she would start up again, but after an hour of peaceful sleep, I got up and walked back to my own bed.

Tomorrow was supposed to be a fresh start for us. She was supposed to start a new school in the morning. Her first day at daycare while I hunted for a job, even if it was just a temporary one.

Looking at the clock on the wall, I wasn't sure that was going to happen now. It was three in the morning, and I knew I wasn't going to sleep anytime soon. I never did after an episode like this.

Being in a new pack was harder than I expected. The smells were different, and San Marco was extremely quiet, especially at this hour.

When I had spoken to Kelsey, the Pack Mother, about moving here, we had agreed to a trial period. Six months. That's all I had committed to.

I knew Kelsey's mate, Kyle Westin, was a powerful but fair Alpha. He cared about shifters and not just his wolves. Westin Pack had become a sanctuary to other shifter types too.

I didn't relish being in a pack again. I hadn't had the best experiences with them in the past and Kyle understood that. I wasn't ready to give my allegiance to him. Still, he let us stay and for that I was extremely grateful because here, I knew without a doubt, we were safe.

We hadn't been safe for a long time. I feared that Vada's night terrors were a result of that, and I hated that I couldn't protect her from them.

Vada had been born into captivity. I didn't know who her biological father was, just a turkey baster of some sort I suppose. As far as I knew she was my biological daughter, but they had run so many experiments on me that I couldn't even be certain of that.

None of it mattered though. Vada was my daughter and that was the end of the story. I would battle to the death anyone who tried to say otherwise.

Our original pack wouldn't even let us return because of the stories that had surfaced of what had gone on inside the Raglan research facilities. Some of it I knew was true, but a lot was just made-up bullshit.

After being rescued from the Raglan, we returned to our pack in New York. I had family there and they were happy to see me but terrified of my little girl. Even my mother turned her back on us, so I had taken my daughter and run far away. Life in the packs weren't necessarily safe for her. There was too much concern and fear over the experiments that had been performed inside the Raglan labs, especially to the children.

In truth, I didn't know what it meant for Vada's future, but the one certainty she would always have is my unconditional love and support. I would do anything for my daughter, and I had, many times, while held in captivity.

I couldn't think about that now. I'd done what I had to do to protect her. I knew that unlike some of the less fortunate kids, aside from the lab work, they had largely left Vada alone. I couldn't let myself regret that, not ever.

Exhausted, I collapsed onto my bed. My eyes had barely closed when I heard her tiny voice.

"Mommy?"

"Yes, sweetheart?"

"I go potty."

I sighed as I pulled the covers back and climbed out of bed. My limbs felt heavy with exhaustion already setting in.

"Come on pumpkin," I said swooping her up in my arms and rushing her to the bathroom.

We were still in the potty-training stage, but I felt like it was almost behind us. Moments like this were momentous, but I was too tired to muster up more than a "Yay, big girl."

"Can I sweep wif you?"

"Of course, pumpkin. Climb up here and snuggle in."

Vada ran her nose across my chest as she fit inside my waiting arms. She sniffed me, smiled, and instantly fell fast asleep.

I kissed the top of her head. "Sweet dreams, baby."

She was so peaceful while I laid awake watching her. As the sun started to rise, I finally began drifting off to sleep.

Much too soon Vada woke up. I was so tired I felt sick to my stomach, but I planted a smile on my face just for her.

"Hi Mommy," she said sweetly as she ran her little hand across my cheek.

"Good morning."

I got her out of bed and to the potty in time. She was really doing great, and I wasn't sure we would need the training pants much longer. We managed to get through breakfast, and I realized she was full of energy and I was completely exhausted.

Checking the time, I realized we could still make it to day care. I hadn't texted them to say she wouldn't be coming and even if I didn't do any job hunting, I could at least get some peaceful rest.

Vada was excited about her new school because I'd been talking it up for days. When I mentioned it to her, she immediately ran and dressed herself, grabbing the little backpack she had picked out.

I looked at my daughter and smiled trying hard not to laugh at the inside out pajama bottoms and the Christmas shirt that was a little too late in the season. It was all complimented by one of my sun hats and a mismatched pair of socks.

"Nice try. How about we slow down and think about this wardrobe choice here."

I picked her up and carried her back to her room where I had already laid out a blue dress with polka dot leggings, matching white socks, and a headband.

She nodded her approval as she made a quick outfit change.

She did get to keep the backpack.

Then we rushed out the door and over to the daycare center. Mary Westin was filling in for the day for Vada's teacher. I knew who she was but hadn't met her yet.

"Hello there, you must be Vada," the older woman said affectionately.

"I'm almost free," she said.

"Three," I corrected.

"Dat wut I say," Vada argued.

"Wow, you are a big girl, aren't you?" Mary said.

Vada proudly nodded her head.

"Come along let me introduce you to my friends."

I watched as they left to go to a classroom down the hall. I wasn't sure if I should follow, leave, or stay put and wait. This was all new territory for me, and I struggled even letting her out of my sight.

I was assured by Kelsey that Vada was safe here and that no one would care about her unique circumstances. I also knew there were other kids born in captivity here so a part of me hoped and prayed she would fit in.

Still, we'd faced rejection before and struggled with finding a home. I refused to get my hopes up that this time things would be different.

Mary returned before I could bring myself to turn and go.

"Hi, Lucy, I'm Mary Westin."

I nodded. "Yes, they let me know that Vanessa wouldn't be in today."

I had already met Vanessa who would be Vada's regular teacher and we'd hit it off well enough. And I'd met Stephanie, the director of the program. I didn't know Mary, but as the former Pack Mother I felt like I should be able to trust her, at least for a few hours. That did nothing to tame my nerves though.

"First time leaving her?" she asked.

"First time ever," I admitted.

"Well, I would say you are much overdue for a break then." Her smile was easy and somehow calming. "You look exhausted dear. Here is my personal cell phone number. When you start to freak out, simply video message this number."

I stared at her in shock as I reached out and took the card from her.

"Won't I interrupt class or something?"

"They're two, Lucy. I think it'll be okay. I was a first-time mom once upon a time too. I still remember how hard it was to let go."

"You're the Alpha's mother, right?"

Her smile brightened proudly. "I am, and I have a whole mess of grandbabies now. I promise you, I'll take good care of her."

I hesitated then slowly nodded. Before I could stop myself, I threw my arms around the woman's neck and hugged her.

"Thank you," I whispered.

It took every ounce of willpower in me to force my legs to move, but I did it. I walked back to the car, sat in the driver's seat and cried.

When the tears had run dry, I drove home, climbed into bed and fell fast asleep.

I awoke several hours later and started to panic. It took me a moment to get my bearings straight and remember where I was, but more importantly where Vada was.

I pulled out my phone and video messaged the number Mary had given me.

I was certain I looked a wild mess, but Mary answered on the second ring with a smile. She put her finger up to her mouth and then turned the camera to show a floor of six sleeping kids, including Vada.

I breathed a sigh of relief.

Mary's face came back onto the screen and gave me a thumbs up.

"Thank you," I mouthed and then disconnected the phone.

She was fine, sleeping soundly even. It suddenly felt like the first normal thing I'd ever experienced with my child.

Micah

Chapter 2

"What is wrong with you?" Grant asked me as I missed the fourth basket in a row.

"I don't know," I admitted. "For some reason my wolf has been restless for days now."

Baine snorted. "You're the doctor, diagnose yourself."

I glared at him as he passed the ball and I shot it right back to him.

I liked the guys on Westin Force, a special ops team of shifters. It was like Westin Pack's own private army.

I'd gotten to work on several missions with them and on Wednesday afternoons, when they weren't out on a job, I joined them for a game of basketball. Today my heart simply wasn't in it.

"Maybe you're coming down with something?" Tarron offered.

I groaned. "I'm not sick, just, I dunno, restless. I don't know how else to describe it."

"When's the last time you went for a run?" Grant asked.

I sighed and tried to think. "Too long, I guess. That's probably all it is."

"You can't let your wolf stay cooped up inside for that long. Just go for a run," he suggested.

My head certainly wasn't in the game, but I still stayed. Even though we were just playing for fun, I hated letting my team down.

When I got subbed out, I sat on the bleachers. I never sat during a game. What was wrong with me?

"Are you sure you're okay?" Tarron asked.

"I'm fine, I guess. Just in a funk today."

"That's not like you, especially on Wednesdays," he pointed out.

It was true. Wednesday was my favorite day of the week. I only took emergency cases on Wednesday and on the weekends. Since my father retired, I was the only true doctor in Westin Pack, though there were some medics and EMTs that could assist when needed, like Grant. He was the field medic for Westin Force's Bravo team, and it wasn't uncommon for us to work together.

Every Wednesday I spent part of my afternoon playing basketball and hanging out with the guys. Then later in the evening it was time for Dungeons and Dragons, my all-time favorite game. I was the local Dungeon Master for my party, or DM as they called me. I knew it was a little dorky, but I just loved it. From the strategy and creativity of developing the game, the story telling, to just spending time with friends, I loved it all. The game meant a lot to me.

"Hey, Susan wants to come check out D&D tonight. Are you cool with that? I really think she'll love it and have been trying to encourage her to come," Tarron told me as he came off the court so I could go back into the game.

Susan was his mate, a fox shifter like Tarron.

"You know I'm cool with that. The more people the more fun."

That wasn't entirely true, there was such a thing as too big of a group, but we weren't anywhere close to that number…yet.

"Are we playing basketball or gossiping, you pussies," Baine said waiting on me.

I just shook my head and rejoined the game.

My head was a mess thinking through how best to add Susan in tonight. Would she want to dive in and play or just observe? Christine was hosting tonight after Quinton had to bail thanks to Kyle calling a Pack Council meeting at the last minute. She hated the thought of anyone knowing she secretly played so we all agreed to be discreet about coming over. I wished I had just offered up my place again. Christine could be a little high maintenance at times, but she had a strategic mind like no other.

Painter passed me the ball. I took my shot and missed.

Baine took the rebound and broke loose as he ran to the other side of the court to easily make his shot without any opponent threat.

"That's eighteen to four. You guys aren't even fun to play with today," he gloated.

"I'm really sorry guys. My head's just not in this game today."

"Yeah, you might as well just leave now and go for that run or something, because you are really sucking ass today," Baine teased as he dribbled the ball more carelessly than usual and then passed it to Silas.

I intercepted the ball with a sudden burst of energy. I didn't have to be the best of the best at the game, but dammit, he wasn't going to call me out like that. With a jump shot from the three point line, I sunk the ball through the net.

"Oh! That had to hurt," Grant mocked.

"Nice," Tarron said.

"Why the hell haven't you been playing like that the whole time then?" Baine asked as I was walking away.

"I'm taking your advice and going for a run. Catch you guys next week… after you've recovered from that one," I added with a hint of mischief in my voice.

Baine had an ego the size of Texas and so all of us took every opportunity possible to put him in his place. I knew he was going to cast a bet that I couldn't do it again or something like that, so I got out of there as fast as I could.

It was rare that anyone got the last word on Baine.

Grant was right. He had to be. I just needed a good run. There was a park outside of town that I often used as a starting point for a run in my wolf form. I drove straight over there, got out of the car, stripped and left my clothes on the backseat, then walked to the edge of the woods.

It wasn't uncommon to see a naked person headed for the woods. If I were to shift with my clothes on, they'd be shredded to pieces, and leaving them out in the open was just asking for someone to take them.

It wasn't that we had a lot of theft in San Marco, but stumbling across a pile of clothes could be considered fair game. Most people wouldn't do that to another, but I'd been on the receiving end of enough pranks in my day to know better. It wasn't worth the risk.

I stretched and looked around the woods as a shiver ran down my spine and I transformed from my human form into my wolf.

Rarely did I give control over to my wolf, but I was so on edge that this time I did just that.

He took off through the woods jumping over logs and running back towards town.

It wasn't really that big of a deal even if my wolf strolled right down Main Street, but it wasn't in my nature to allow myself to be that exposed.

I lived in the largest wolf shifter pack in the world. No one would think twice about seeing a wolf around. Even local human tourists were aware of the possibility as there were wildlife preserve signs posted along the road leading up to San Marco.

Just as I was about to rein my wolf in, he veered east, away from town. I allowed him to continue his run as I was lost in my own thoughts.

It felt great to be out in my fur for a bit, yet for some reason, my wolf still felt on edge.

We ran on through a creek, between some boulders going deeper and deeper into the forest, and then he changed directions again. There was something in the air that had caught his full attention. I had to admit, I was a little curious about what was distracting him off the trail we were running.

Suddenly he came to an abrupt halt at the edge of the woods, crouched down and stared at a small single-story home just in view. It was nestled pretty deep in the woods, and I didn't recognize it. My wolf whimpered and sort of crawled closer to the house in a submissive form I'd never seen from him.

I had no idea who lived there. It could be anyone really, and while I didn't feel like we were stalking anything, the same motion could have been my wolf on the hunt. That had to be it. I just hoped it wasn't a skunk in the area this time.

Suddenly the door opened, and a very young girl toddled outside.

My wolf stood and howled. It startled the child who turned and ran back inside. It had caught me off guard too.

I could see someone standing at the window watching me, but I couldn't make them out.

I wasn't certain just how far we had run off course though I knew from the scent that I was still in pack territory, but there was something else there that I was certain I had never smelled before.

An odd feeling washed over me and gave me an uneasy sensation in my gut.

I regained control and then forced my wolf to turn and run back. Normally I was in perfect sync with my wolf, but not this time. He was angry and aggressive. I didn't like it, and I had no idea what to do about it, so I just kept running in the direction I thought was my best route back.

It took a while, and the sun was starting to set when I smelled familiar scents around me and knew I was close to the park where I'd left my car.

I shifted back to my human form and walked the remainder of the way. My wolf roared in my head for it too. I still had no idea what had set him off, but it was clear he was not happy.

Dressing quickly, I slid into the driver's seat and frowned. I didn't feel any better after that run. If anything, I felt worse.

I only had an hour before I was due at Christine's. We'd all agreed to eat before arriving, so I swung into town stopping by the Crate for a burger and fries.

"What are you drinking tonight?" Jesse asked.

"Just a Coke. I have someplace to be."

"Oh, I'm aware. Sally Merchant's been trying to get Misty to join your little group, but Wednesday is Hump Day and things get a little crazy around here. I can't be short staffed."

"I'll mention it to Sally. Or you could finally hire on another set of hands and give the poor woman a break," I said boldly.

"Yeah, yeah, yeah. I've been thinking about it. If you know of anyone looking for a job, send them my way. I'll consider it. But not just so Misty can go to your game night."

"Of course not," I said with a grin.

"I mean it, Micah."

"I know. You really are shorthanded here, Jesse. Business has been picking up with all the new shifters in town and who knows how long it will take before the Force finds places to relocate them."

It wasn't just Jesse's bar that was staying busy, I'd had a significant influx of patients since Westin Force had disbanded a large Raglan encampment and rescued thousands of shifters being held captive there. Several hundred of them had nowhere to go and were temporarily taking residence at the Lodge just outside Pack territory. There was no way of knowing just how long they would be with us.

I finished my meal and said goodbye. I needed to swing by the house to pick up my stuff before heading over to Christine's place.

*****

"You're late," Christine declared as she opened the door and then looked around behind me to make certain no one saw me come in. "You're never late."

I sighed. "Sorry. I had to eat dinner and was talking to Jesse, and I just got tied up."

"You were leaving the Crate when I headed over here," Sally said.

I glared at her. "I had to stop by the house and pick stuff up for tonight."

"Well, it sure took you long enough."

I threw my hands up in exasperation. "Sorry."

"What's wrong, man?" Jeremiah asked.

"Nothing," I snapped. "Why does everyone keep asking me that?"

"Maybe because you're on edge and you're normally one of the most even tempered people we know?" Christine offered.

I tried to pull it together. I didn't mean to take my foul mood out on them. I knew I just needed to get lost in the story far away from this world.

I set out the maps and pulled out my notebook containing much of my storyboard and notes. By now everyone was bringing their own polyhedral dice to play with though I pulled out a set of my own to make available just in case. One could never have enough dice.

"Now, where did we leave off?"

"Glendore was about to battle the green orc," Tarron said.

"Oh, I can't wait to see how this turns out," Sally added excitedly.

"Okay then, let's get started." I called the game into play. My heart wasn't entirely in it, but I knew I would soon be lost to a world of magic and fantasy.

Lucy

Chapter 3

"It's just a formality to appease the state," Vanessa explained. "Sorry I wasn't here yesterday to get everything sorted for you."

"It's fine. So she just needs a physical?"

"Afraid so. The state mandates it and since we are technically considered an early childhood education center and not just a daycare, it's just easier to follow the human rules to the T. Trust me, I get it. She's a shifter and her odds of being sick or having any ailments at all are pretty slim, but really what does it hurt? Doc's used to this protocol and knows exactly what to do."

She handed me a form and smiled.

"Just take that down to the clinic along with Vada, of course, and you'll be in and out in no time. She can come right back to school when it's over." She gave me some quick directions to the clinic as I tried to memorize them. It didn't seem too hard.

I sighed. "Okay. Thanks. Come on sweetie, let's get this over with."

I was a little irritated that no one had mentioned this, but if I were ever going to find a job around here then I needed Vada to be in a safe place I could count on to care for her.

I toted her back to the car, buckled her in, and climbed in for the short drive to the clinic following the directions Vanessa had given me.

Of course I got to the first intersection and couldn't remember if I was supposed to go left or right. I didn't know what to do and I was so exasperated that I just wanted to sit there and cry.

Why couldn't something be easy for once?

Some older women were approaching on the sidewalk. I rolled my window down and leaned over.

"Excuse me, I think I'm lost. Can you help?"

"Oh dear, where are you headed?" the short plump one asked.

"I'm looking for the clinic."

She eyed me suspiciously. No doubt she knew I wasn't from around here.

"I'm Lucy and this is my daughter, Vada. We're new to the area." I explained to hopefully ward off their suspicions.

"Vada? This is little Vada, the namesake of our Vada?" the woman asked.

"Um, yes?"

It was a safe bet, I mean how many Vadas could there possibly be in San Marco?

I cringed thinking of how I hadn't even reached out and told Vada we were moving here. I suddenly felt horrible for that. She had done so much for the both of us while in captivity.

"I'm Tarron's Nonna. He works with Silas, Vada's mate," she informed me.

I gave her a confused look. I had met Vada's mate and his team during the big rescue. I vaguely remembered Tarron but could have sworn he was the fox shifter. One sniff told me this woman was a wolf. I knew I must have him confused with someone else, but I forced a smile and nodded.

"Yes, of course. It's so nice to meet you."

The old lady beamed. “You and your daughter will have to come to dinner sometime soon.”

“That would be great,” I managed to say just trying to placate the woman. I needed directions, not dinner. “But can you help me with the clinic?”

“Oh yes, of course, dear. Just make a right here and go down a little ways. It’s just down about a mile on the left.”

“Right then on the left,” I repeated.

“You’ve got it. Good luck.”

Before she could say any more, I gave her a thanks, rolled up the window and drove off. I had been so close it was downright embarrassing.

I pulled into a parking spot and sat there blowing out a deep breath. I was irritated with myself as much as the situation as I unstrapped Vada from the car and set her down. I was halfway to the door when I remembered the paperwork.

“Argh!”

I ran back to retrieve it while Vada stood watching me by the door.

I was back in a flash, feeling even more off kilter than I had before.

My wolf was restless. We’d been in the territory for several days now, and I thought it was improving, then yesterday afternoon a wolf came near the house Kyle had offered us to stay in and ever since my wolf had been downright aggressive. The weird thing was that we were around wolves in the area all the time, but this one she clearly had issues with.

I had been anxious and jittery ever since.

As we walked into the clinic, my wolf tried to surge in much the same as she had done with the wolf. I was not happy about it.

There was no one working the front desk and no one in the waiting room.

I banged on the little bell.

"Just a minute," a deep, very male, voice yelled from the back somewhere.

Something slammed into me at the sound, and I felt embarrassingly and uncomfortably wet.

What the hell was happening to me?

"Sorry about that. I've been a little distracted today. What can I do for…" he paused and stared at me with wide eyes as shocked as I felt. "You," he whispered almost reverently.

Mate! my wolf cried out in the back of my head.

"No!" I screamed, grabbing up my daughter and running from the building.

It wasn't until I reached the car that I realized my keys were sitting on top of the paperwork back in the clinic.

For a solid minute I contemplated walking home, packing, and leaving.

This couldn't be happening. I couldn't have a mate. I didn't want a mate. There was so much broken inside of me that I could never take a mate. It wouldn't be right.

And then there was Vada. How could I expect any man to accept her when my own family couldn't?

I was freaking out so badly that I didn't notice when he walked outside carrying my keys.

"You, uh, forgot these," he said.

I stared down at the keys feeling as if there was a great chasm stretched out between us. I could see the uncertainty in his eyes, too.

As I took them, he didn't look my way. Instead, he crouched down to Vada's height and held out his hand.

"Hi, I'm Micah, or Doc if you prefer. You must be Vada. Vanessa called and said I should expect you to stop by."

Vada giggled and then shook his hand. Despite everything she'd been through, she was still so open and mostly innocent with people.

"I understand you are such a big girl that you're ready for big girl school."

She grinned and nodded.

"I am. I big girl."

"Yes, you are."

He sat down on the ground in front of her and pulled out a stethoscope.

"Do you know what this is?"

I braced for her reaction. She'd seen too many of those in her short lifetime, but like the champ she was, she didn't even flinch, quite the opposite even.

She nodded her head as her eyes lit with excitement.

"You are a big girl. Can I listen to your heart with it?"

"Yes, pease."

He placed it on her heart and listened then checked all her vitals being careful to explain each thing he was doing first. By the end of the very odd visit, he had Vada laughing and then sang the ABCs with her as he filled out her paperwork.

Finally, he stood and faced me.

"She's perfect," he said handing me the paper.

Vada surprised me and held her arms up asking him to pick her up. He did so without hesitation.

"Miss Vada, you're going to do great in school. Tell your mommy that she has absolutely nothing to worry about."

He passed my child back to me. His hands brushed against my skin in the process, and it felt like I'd just touched a powerline.

Mine! my wolf growled in my head.

I was trying hard not to hyperventilate. Why was this happening now?

After talking to Kelsey, I had hope that just maybe Vada and I would be safe here, happy even. I knew it was too much to ask to be fully accepted, but I wanted to be functional within this Pack at the very least.

Now, I didn't know what to do.

I stared at him, really looking at him this time. He was handsome. Tall, but lean. I was drawn to him in ways I couldn't even understand, not like I had been with any other man I'd ever met.

Mate! my wolf reminded me, and I practically growled.

Of course I knew that was the only reason, but it sure didn't feel like it in that moment.

Most important to me, he was kind. He'd been sweeter to my daughter than anyone ever had before. I wanted to cry.

I needed to get away.

I realized we'd been standing there staring at each other awkwardly for an undetermined amount of time.

"Is that it?" I finally blurted out.

"I suppose so," he said, almost sadly, and I felt like there was more meaning behind his simple words.

I couldn't bring my feet to move though. I was frozen in place.

He pulled something from his pocket and then handed it to me.

"Most kids around here rarely if ever get sick, but if you have any concerns and need to discuss something, here's my contact info."

I looked down at his business card and knew with certainty we weren't just talking about Vada now.

My wolf seemed so certain that he was our mate. I couldn't tell if he felt the same though. Was it possible to have a one-sided mating?

My head was spinning in confusion and my body uncomfortable in my own skin.

"Okay," I said softly.

I forced myself to walk away as I carried Vada to the car and buckled her in.

"Thank you," I said feeling uncomfortably out of sorts.

"Micah," he said.

"I know," I blurted out.

Silence stretched between us for what felt like an eternity. Once again, I thought my feet had been glued to the ground.

"And you are?" he finally asked.

"Lucy," I managed without sounding like a complete idiot.

I didn't want to like him. I didn't want to get to know him. I just wanted to get as far away from this man as possible, yet my feet wouldn't move.

He smirked as if he knew it, too.

That look should have pissed me off, but if I was being honest with myself, all it did was endear him to me.

"Um, okay. Bye," I said forcing my feet to me.

"Lucy?" he asked.

"Yeah?"

He seemed to be biting back a grin. "Your paperwork."

I turned my head and noticed it was sitting on the roof of the car. I hadn't even realized I set it down but must have while I buckled Vada into her seat.

"Right. Right, uh, thanks."

I grabbed the paperwork and like a big fat chicken, I jumped into the driver's seat and got the hell out of there.

My head was still swimming in disbelief as I returned Vada to school and went home to curl up into a ball and cry for all the things I knew I could never have, because above everything else, I had to protect Vada. No one could know the truth about her conception and Doctor Micah threatened that very thing.

I could never be intimate with a man because I would never deny Vada as my biological daughter, but how could I explain that I had children yet had never been with a man.

My own mother had called her an abomination and I couldn't bear to hear those words again, not from anyone, but especially not from my one true mate.

I choked on a sob. He was a doctor of all things. He'd surely know the truth if I ever gave in to the mating call I was feeling.

Micah

Chapter 4

It had happened. I met my one true mate, and she was already taken.

Mine! my wolf growled at the thought.

I had recognized the little girl immediately. She was the one at the house in the woods. My wolf had known our mate was there.

What had I done in this life to deserve a mated mate?

How was this even possible?

I stood on the curb and watched her drive away remembering the gut punch of devastation that had hit me when she yelled "No!" and ran from my office.

Of course she said no, she was the mother of a two year old. She clearly already had a mate and no matter what my wolf told me, she could never be mine.

Tarron stopped by at that exact moment.

I wasn't sure what I looked like staring longingly as my mate drove away, but it was enough to make my friend jump from his car and run to my side.

"Are you okay? What happened?"

"I'm fine," I managed to say, forcing myself to turn and walk back into my clinic.

Tarron followed.

"You don't look okay, man. You look like you've just seen a ghost."

I snorted at the irony. Maybe I had.

"Have you ever wondered what would happen if you chose a compatible mate? I mean before you met Susan. Like if you had and then met her, would your fox have recognized her as your true mate?"

"I don't have a clue why we're talking about this, but I don't think that's how it works. Once a bond is made your spirit animal shouldn't look or want any other woman."

"So what about her then? What if she wasn't mated and crossed paths with you, her true mate, only you're already mated to someone else. Would she recognize you as her true mate?"

He growled clearly upset by the question.

"I don't know, Micah. Maybe? Why?"

"Because I just crossed paths with my true mate, and she's already mated."

"What? No way."

I gave him a sad look. I didn't know what to do. My wolf was already pining for Lucy. Could I even stay away from her?

"What am I going to do, Tarron?"

"I'm sorry man, I didn't even know this was possible."

"Me either, but I can already feel the pull to her. I can't stay here."

"What?"

"I don't know if I'm strong enough to stay away," I confessed.

"Then challenge his ass."

"And hurt her? She made her choice."

I turned the open sign to closed and locked up.

"What are you going to do?"

"Leave," I said simply. "I have to."

I was a doctor. I believed in science, not miracles and true love, yet my heart had instantly changed its rhythmic pattern to match hers the second I laid eyes on the beautiful woman my wolf wanted to claim.

It was just my luck really. I would spend eternity longing for a woman I could never have.

The thing was, I had an obligation to the Pack. I knew Grant could take over in the interim and I was certain they would find a new Pack physician. Heck, my father might even come out of retirement to pitch in once I explained my situation.

My heart dropped. I'd blurted it out to Tarron in a moment of shock. No one else could know.

"You can't mention this to anyone!"

"What? You want to keep this a secret?"

"Tarron, I don't even think she felt the connection. It was entirely one-sided, and I do not want to upset her life with her chosen mate. It's not her fault, we literally just met."

"How is it even possible that you just met someone if they are here in the Pack. You know everyone and everything around here."

"Not her," I said. "Look it doesn't matter. You can't tell anyone."

"Well, if you leave, people are going to ask."

"Then tell them you know nothing. I could probably get my hands on some of the memory erasing serum the Force uses on occasion."

"You know about that?"

"Of course I know about that. What did you say? I know everything around here."

Tarron groaned. I knew he hated his words being thrown back in his face.

"No one," I said again.

"What are you going to tell Kyle?"

"I don't know yet. I should get over there now. I have to pack. You'll take over for me as DM right? I'll drop all the stuff you need off on my way out of town."

"I think you're being ridiculous. Do you even know her name?"

"Of course I know her name."

"So who's her mate then?"

I paused. "I don't know," I blurted out. "And I'd rather not find out."

"Then how do you know she even has one?"

"Because she has a toddler," I said.

"Oh."

"Yeah, oh. There are certain things you need in order to make that happen."

"I mean technically you don't have to have an actual mate. Are you sure she's even mated?"

I glared at him. But was I? No. Could I handle knowing who her mate was? Whose face she woke up to every morning? Who… I shook my head. I couldn't let myself go down that path.

"I have to go. Lock up when you leave."

I pushed past Tarron, got in my car and drove straight to the Alpha House.

*****

Mary Westin still lived at Alpha House with her mate, Jason. They were the former Alpha and Pack Mother before the torch had been passed to Kyle and Kelsey who chose to live elsewhere in the territory.

When I knocked on the door, Mary answered.

"Micah? Is everything okay?"

"Fine. I don't know. Is Kyle here?"

"Yes, he's in his office."

I didn't even wait to be invited in. I pushed past her with a quick, "thanks."

I knew the place well and knew exactly where Kyle's office was. I wouldn't say we were exactly friends, but I had known the Alpha my entire life and had helped deliver both of his boys.

I knocked harder than I meant to.

"Enter," I heard Kyle's voice boom.

I opened the door and walked in.

"Micah? Did we have an appointment I missed?"

"No, sir. I just need a moment of your time and then I'll be on my way."

I started to pace back and forth across his office, a clear sign that my wolf was on edge.

"Do you want to sit?"

"No, I'd rather stand."

"Okay, how about you tell me what's going on then."

"I'm leaving the Pack," I blurted out.

"What? Why?"

He seemed incredibly calm for the bombshell I'd just dropped on him. Too calm. It made me even more agitated.

"Micah, tell me what's happened."

"I don't want to discuss it. I just need to leave, immediately. I'm not coming back, Kyle. I haven't spoken with Grant or my father, but I am sure between the two of them they can work out something until you find a replacement."

"Why?" he demanded.

I shook my head. "It doesn't matter, this is my choice."

I felt a tingling sensation and my body started to feel heavy as I struggled to stay standing.

"You're using Alpha powers on me?"

I hadn't considered this possibility.

"Tell me," he demanded again.

My knees nearly buckled under the weight of his stare.

"I met my true mate," I blurted out.

The pressure was instantly lifted.

"Well, that's wonderful. I hadn't heard. Congratulations."

I tried not to cringe, but my face must have shown my distress and he quirked one eyebrow up as he watched me carefully.

"Is there some reason she cannot move here to Westin Pack instead?"

I didn't want to answer, but once more I felt the weight of his powers.

"She's already here," I admitted.

"Micah, are you scared?"

"What? No!"

"Look, I get it. Both my sisters ran from their true mates too. It's a crazy time. Your emotions are on a rollercoaster, and no one can prepare you for this. I promise, she's worth it."

"You don't understand," I finally said collapsing onto one of the chairs.

"Then tell me."

I didn't want to, but I had to.

"She's already taken another mate."

"What? No, that can't be."

"I wish it weren't true, but there are certain biological factors that say otherwise."

"Who is she? I thought you knew everyone in the Pack."

"I thought so too. I think she recently moved here," I answered successfully avoiding his question.

I could tell Kyle was racking his brain trying to figure it out.

"But who is she, Micah?"

I shook my head.

"You don't know, or you don't want to tell me?"

"A little of both," I told him honestly.

"I need a name."

I shook my head.

"Don't make me use my Alpha powers again," he threatened.

Still, I stubbornly refused until the pressure resurfaced once more.

"Kyle please."

"I need a name."

"Lucy," I finally managed. "Her name is Lucy, but that's all I know."

"Lucy? Does she have a young daughter?"

I nodded. "Vada."

He paused, and then rubbed his temples.

"Jesus, Micah."

"I know. And I'm going to do the right thing by them, Kyle, I swear. I just can't stay here. I had always assumed that if a true mate took a compatible mate that the mating bond would supersede a true mate calling. In all my years of practicing medicine for shifters, I've never heard of this happening."

He gave me a pitying look. "I don't think that's how it works."

"Clearly, which is why I have to leave."

"No, you don't understand me. Look, I was going to have this conversation with you in full confidence as Pack physician. I promised Lucy I wouldn't say anything to anyone though. You were going to be the exception just so you are aware of the situation and can help keep an eye on things."

"What are you talking about?"

"Shit. You've really put me in a bind here, Micah."

"Just tell me. You were going to tell me anyway."

"Yeah, as an impartial and respected doctor, not as a mating male."

"You know what, don't tell me. It will be easier that way. Just approve my leave and let me get the hell away from this place, from her."

"That's not going to happen, Micah."

"Kyle, please be reasonable. I'm not trying to cause trouble here. This is as much for my own self-preservation as it is about protecting her. You cannot condemn me to stay here longing for a woman I cannot have. I don't think I'm strong enough not to go to her and we both know what a disaster that would be. If you do not release me, no other Alpha will take me in. I'll be forced to live my remaining days alone in the human realm. Are you really prepared to do that? You know scientifically speaking that we were not created to be lone wolves."

He burst out laughing. "Micah, I had no idea you could be so dramatic. Let me put you out of your misery. Lucy isn't mated."

I froze and my jaw dropped. "What did you say?"

"She is not mated."

"But her daughter…"

He squirmed in his seat uncomfortably. "Her daughter is what I was going to discuss with you. How much do you know about your mate?"

My heart raced. *My mate.* My Alpha had just acknowledged her as my mate.

"Nothing. She brought Vada into the clinic today for a school physical. When our eyes met, she freaked out and left. I followed. I managed to make it through the assessment of her daughter without entirely making an ass of myself. Kyle she's not yet three years old. Where the hell is her father?"

I had jumped out of my chair at some point in the rant and began pacing again.

He sighed. "Take a seat, Micah. If it were anyone else, I'd be telling you to just go and talk to her. And if you were anyone else, I'd certainly not be sharing this."

Curiosity had me taking a seat.

"I'm not speaking to you as her potential mate right now. I'm talking to you as their doctor and what I'm going to tell you absolutely falls under patient-doctor confidentiality. Do you understand?"

"Yes, sir," I said.

"And can you do that, Micah? Can you separate your personal feelings from your professional ones right now?"

"I don't know," I said honestly. "But I damn well do know I'm not leaving this room until you tell me."

He nodded slowly. “Lucy doesn’t have a mate. She is one of the Raglan victims from the big rescue.” He paused letting that sink in as a growl escaped me.

“Sorry. I’m okay, continue, please.”

“Her daughter is literally named after Silas’s Vada who delivered her into this world.”

“How long was Lucy in captivity?” I asked.

“Five years I believe she said.”

“So Vada was conceived in captivity then?” I asked.

“Micah, Vada was *created* in captivity.”

He let that sink in for a minute, know I was well aware of the experiments that had been run on shifters while with the Raglan. I had poured over the data and details in preparation to receive over two hundred of them here. I knew most of their cases. How had Lucy and Vada escaped me?

“I can see the confusion on your face. You’re mentally going through all of their files, aren’t you?”

I shrugged but we both knew he was correct.

“She just arrived.”

“How is that possible?” Now I was dying to know everything there was to know about her and the child.

“She’s a bit skittish, Micah.”

“Oh, I’ve already experienced that for myself.”

I was surprisingly calm with the news. My freak out was over. She wasn’t mated. She was mine. That’s all I could think about. She was mine.

“She originated from the New York Pack, and she still has family there, so after the big rescue, she went home.”

The way his voice changed I knew what was coming next.

“They didn’t accept her back?” I guessed.

“No, they did. They just didn’t accept her kid. You have to understand, the New York Pack was very closely affected by the experiments, especially with the babies. Abominations is what they call them. From what I gather she moved home with her mother.”

"Her own mother rejected her?"

"Afraid so. She didn't stay there long and had been moving around within the human world until Kelsey personally reached out to check on her. As you know we have a team doing that to ensure these people are integrating back into their lives without further assistance needed. For those that need the help we have an assistance fund. Anyway, when Kelsey reached out to Lucy, she sort of broke down. The two connected and Kels convinced her to move here where we assured her she could have a fresh start for the both of them."

"As in no one knows the truth."

"Exactly. I can't even fathom the feelings of people calling my child an abomination. So she didn't have a normal conception. There are a lot worse things in this world. Around here every child matter and we've tried to explain that to her, but quite frankly, she's scared, Micah."

"It's not like we haven't seen it before, though. Ben and Shelby's triplets potentially have a similar story. I've been watching them since birth, and they are growing and maturing just as any other normal kid."

"I know. We haven't really discussed any of that with her yet. She even asked us not to mention to Vada that she is here."

"She's scared," I said.

"And very much alone."

Lucy

Chapter 5

I had my cry and then I got up and cleaned the house. Having things neat and orderly had always helped me settle emotionally.

I also packed a bag. Then I unpacked it. Finally, I packed it again.

I knew I had some big decisions to make, but I was still in shock. I stared down at his card in my hand. I was itching to call him even knowing that was the dumbest thing ever.

I barely met the guy. I shouldn't be feeling all these things for him.

Mate!

That was it. It wasn't him; it was the idea of him. I was simply mourning the idea of never having a mate, not him. I wasn't mourning him. I didn't even know him, and he could never know me, not in that way.

I was startled when there was a knock at the door.

I couldn't imagine who it might be.

There was no one I knew or even wanted to talk to. If there was a problem at the school then Vanessa would have called me first. I just pretended I wasn't home.

When the knock came a second time, I stepped back into the shadows as if they could somehow see I was there even though I was not by the window.

The third knock, I crouched down on the floor with an uneasy feeling.

You're an adult, Lucy. This is ridiculous. Grow some balls. You are no victim. I pep talked myself.

With a huff of resolution, I walked over and opened the door.

My jaw dropped. Micah was the last person I expected to see here.

"What are you doing here?" I asked.

"We need to talk."

He pushed into the house leaving me no choice in the matter. I should have been furious. I should have demanded he leave right this instant. I didn't and secretly, I liked his assertive attitude.

I used to be that way. I would tackle the world head on. My mother used to say there was nothing I couldn't do when I set my mind to something. Micah reminded me of that. But I wasn't that person anymore.

Now, I was scared and pathetic. I was broken beyond repair, and I couldn't bring him down with me. I already worried enough about the effects it would have on Vada.

He looked down and noticed the bags.

"Are you leaving?" he asked.

"I don't know," I told him honestly.

He sighed. "Don't blame you."

"What?"

"I tried to leave too. I'm sorry. I didn't exactly handle things well earlier."

There was no point in denying it, he was obviously going to address the whole mating thing.

"You handled things great with my daughter today. That means a lot to me."

"I tried to leave too," he confessed.

"What? Why?"

He shrugged. "Made assumptions I probably shouldn't have."

I nodded understanding. "You figured I was mated already."

"I did. I begged Kyle to allow me to leave."

"Why would you need his permission?"

"Westin Pack is the largest pack in the world. If I left without his approval, no other Pack would take me in. We aren't designed to be lone wolves, Lucy."

Hearing my name roll off his tongue caused a shiver to run down my spine. I could feel myself growing wet again. This was a terrible reaction when I was trying to be bold and face things like an adult. It certainly was not helping the situation any.

He sniffed the air, and a slight smile tipped the corners of his lips.

Oh no. He can smell my arousal. I was so embarrassed.

"So, as you can imagine, I really needed his permission," he said as if nothing had just happened.

"And did he give it to you?" I asked because I had no idea what else to say.

"No." He frowned.

"No?"

"No. But you do understand I am the Pack physician here, right? The only Pack physician?"

"Yes." I didn't know where he was going with all of this.

"As such, I'm privy to things other people aren't. It's all doctor-patient privilege stuff."

I could feel the color draining from my face. Kyle told him. I knew it before he could even say anything further.

"Lucy."

"Don't. He shouldn't have told you."

"He only told me what I needed to hear."

"He had no right."

"He's the Alpha. He has every right."

I pursed my lips and crossed my arms completely horrified. If he knew, why was he even here?

"What are you doing here, Micah? Really? If it's just to say, I'm sorry you're so screwed up and your daughter's an abomination, then do us both a favor and get out of my house right now."

I was furious. Somewhere deep down I knew Kyle had mentioned sharing Vada's unique case with the Pack physician so he could keep an eye on things as she grew, but I didn't know that same guy would be my one true mate.

"I get you're hurt, Lucy, but I'm not a complete asshole. And I would never think those things, let alone say them."

Tears were starting to burn the rims of my eyes, but I would not cry in front of him.

"Do you really want to know what I thought as he explained your situation to me?"

I shook my head. I didn't want to hear it.

"Well, too bad because the only thing I truly cared about in everything he shared with me was she's not mated. There's a chance. You know damn well, you're my true mate. I can see the panic that causes you, smell your…"

"Don't say it!"

He smirked. "I was going to say anxiety, but that too."

I groaned.

"Lucy, Vada is a smart, beautiful, thriving toddler. You're doing great with her."

The tears broke free. How I had longed to hear someone else acknowledge my maternal skills. Vada was amazing and perfect in every way as far as I was concerned, but to hear a complete stranger agree was overwhelming me.

Micah walked over and wrapped his arms around me and held me tight. I felt safe in his arms, safe for the first time in years.

"If Kyle really told you my story, you wouldn't be here right now."

"Give me some credit. I've been working with cases just like yours for years now, Lucy. Sadly, this isn't something new or even shocking to me. I've heard these stories before. I won't say I'm unaffected by them because that would honestly make me a pretty shitty doctor, but I'm not surprised or freaking out to hear it."

I sobbed harder and when I felt so weak that my legs nearly buckled under me, he held me tighter and lifted me up again.

"I'm so sorry. I will live every day regretting not being there for you."

I pulled back to look him in the face completely caught off guard. "What?"

"I should have protected you from this."

"Micah, you didn't even know I existed."

"I knew my true mate was out there and I did absolutely nothing to find you. You're my mate, Lucy, that's my number one job in this world. It's what I was created to do."

I shook my head. "Don't be ridiculous. Nothing that happened to me was your fault."

He cradled my face in his hands and forced me to look at him.

"And it wasn't yours either."

I knew then that I had just walked right into that.

"No one can know about Vada."

"If that's what you want, I'll honor that."

"You don't understand. She terrifies people."

"She's just a baby."

"I know that, but others, they just don't get it. I mean seriously, have you ever worked with a child that was genetically engineered in a lab?"

It hurt me to even say the words aloud.

"Yes."

"Huh?"

"I said yes. The Raglan were monsters, and they did a lot of horrible things to a lot of people, Lucy. I told you, I've been dealing with the fall out for years."

I knew there were kids like Vada out there. I'd even assisted in delivering a few, but I hadn't expected him to know about them.

"Look, we have a family here who adopted three of them, triplets. They are all Vada's age."

"Alice," I whispered.

"Alice? You mean Mary Alice? So you already know Shelby and Ben's kids?"

"What? No. Well maybe. Sort of."

He chuckled. "Okay?"

"Alice and I were pregnant at the same time in the same facility. There was an attack or something. I don't know. I thought she'd died, but during the big rescue I'd heard her babies had survived. One of the men that saved us adopted them. I had forgotten all about that. They're here?"

He grinned down at me and nodded. "They are and they are thriving almost three-year-olds, just like your daughter."

"Vada was born that day, too."

"I didn't know that."

"You're really not freaked out by her?"

"Never."

"Are those other babies here? They're really here in Westin Pack?" I repeated.

His smiled warmed me from the inside.

"They really are. I'll be happy to introduce you to Shelby."

"And the Pack accepts them?"

"They do. Kyle would honestly banish anyone who called them an abomination."

Another sob escaped me. It was hard to comprehend what I was hearing.

Vada wasn't the only one.

I suddenly realized I was still standing in his arms. He was so far into my personal space that my fight or flight instincts should have kicked in.

I took a step back making things awkward between us.

"Sorry," I mumbled.

He shoved his hands in his pockets. Whether it was intentional or not, that small motion made my heart flutter and I felt somehow unimaginably safer with this man.

Micah

Chapter 6

Lucy had let me hold her and comfort her. It was so much more than I had imagined possible when I left Kyle's place and drove around until I found the house I'd seen from the woods.

Now that she had taken a step back and severed our physical connection, I felt cold and empty inside. I wanted to feel her warmth surrounding me again. I could quickly become addicted to it, to her.

I wasn't thinking when I left Kyle's place and drove straight to Lucy's even though he had sworn me to secrecy and explained how she didn't want anyone to know.

So what did I do?

I went to her and blabbed it all like a big idiot.

I was lucky she hadn't already kicked me out, especially the way I had held her so close to me while she was vulnerable. I certainly hadn't expected her to open up to me in any way, not yet at least. It was far more than I had a right to ask for.

I was pretty certain I hadn't done anything inappropriate. Had she even noticed when I sniffed her hair? I was a wolf, that shouldn't have been too out of the ordinary. Well, I hoped not at least.

Being so close to her had turned me on something fierce. When she awkwardly put space between us, I feared maybe my desire for her had been a little too clear. I didn't dare glance down to check and see if my pants were tented though, at least not when she was still looking in my direction.

We stood there staring at each other and I doubted either of us truly knew what to say next.

An alarm suddenly sounded making us both jump.

Lucy pulled out her phone and gave me a sad smile.

"Sorry, but that's my reminder that it's time to go and pick up Vada from school."

"Right. I should probably check on my clinic. I'm expected to hold office hours today, and well, I sorta closed the place down after you left. It was a moment of panic."

"Would you really have just left?"

"I thought you were mated to someone else, so, yes, I really would have. There was no way I could meet you and not be able to see you and touch you. If you were already mated that wasn't going to be possible."

She gave me a quirky look. "And just because I'm not, you think that's going to happen?"

I felt a sharp stab of pain in my chest and recognized it once again as rejection. I couldn't falter that easily though.

I winked at her as a huge smile enveloped my face. It was the kind of look most women swooned over.

"I guess we'll see. I'm feeling like just maybe I've got a bit of stalker in me."

She snorted trying not to laugh. "That was terrible."

I shrugged. "Maybe, but I'll see you tomorrow."

I left before she could tell me no. I wasn't going to try and force a relationship on her, but I also knew that now that I'd met her, there was no way I was going to be able to stay away. I might have to get creative with ideas for ways to make that happen.

For now, all I really wanted was a chance to get to know her and for her to get to know me too.

I didn't think that was too much to ask for. Only time would tell.

*****

True to my word, I swung by Lucy's over my lunch break the next day. I had been surprisingly anxious all morning but began to calm down on the drive over knowing I was about to see my mate.

I jumped out of the car and walked up her porch to knock on the door. My hands were sweaty, and I realized I was nervous. Things were still up in the air between us. I had no idea how she was feeling about finding out I was her one true mate.

I knocked on the door.

There was no answer.

I waited, looking around, and realizing her car wasn't there either. How I hadn't noticed that driving up was beyond me. I was seriously losing it.

I had brought lunch for the two of us.

My stomach grumbled so I went and retrieved the meal from my car and sat on her front steps. As I was pulling out the sandwiches I'd made that morning, a car pulled up.

Lucy sat there looking at me almost confused and then slowly got out of the car.

"You're here."

"I don't know why that surprises you. I told you I'd see you today."

"I know. I just didn't think you meant it."

"Well, you'll learn I never say things I don't mean. Are you hungry?"

"Uh, yeah, I am."

I wasn't prepared for how happy that made me, because I knew I could take care of her, even if only in a small way.

"I brought lunch. Want to join me?"

"Okay," she said hesitantly as if she wasn't sure what to do or expect.

She sat down next to me, and the small width of the stairs meant our knees touched. There was such a sense of calm that small touch gave me that I just stared at her in wonder.

"What?"

"Nothing," I said.

I reached into the bag and pulled out a sub sandwich to hand her. Next, I produced two containers of pasta salad, some grapes, raw carrots, and two small bags of chips. I had to hunt for the forks and napkins I knew I had remembered to pack. Finally, I offered her a choice of water, soda, or tea to drink.

"Tea."

I made a mental note of what she liked with a little smile quirking my lips. Tea was my favorite too and just in case she chose it, I had packed two bottles.

She bit into her sandwich and moaned. I stared at her with my own sub frozen halfway to my mouth as I gulped hard.

"Sorry. I was hungrier than I thought, and this is delicious. Where did you get it from?"

I felt ridiculously happy that she liked it.

"I made it this morning."

"You made this?"

"Yup." I gave her a sheepish grin.

"Micah, this is the best thing I've had since I got here. This is amazing."

"Wait until you try my famous pasta salad."

Her eyes sparkled with excitement as she set the sandwich down and dove into the pasta.

Even though I was more prepared for it this time, the little whimpers of appreciation as she ate made me uncomfortably hard. My mind transported to places it shouldn't as I wondered just what sort of noises she'd make in bed.

"So, busy morning?" I stupidly said just trying to change the subject to anything that didn't make me think of Lucy naked.

"Vada had an accident at school so I had to run in a change of clothes. I brought two just in case it happens again."

"Potty training?"

"Yes. She's so close, but she's still only two and this was rare for her."

"Two is still early. It's not uncommon for kids to not be able to hold it at her age, and even older. A lot of the time during the day they just get so busy and into whatever they are doing that they ignore the signs until it's too late. She'll get there."

She nudged me with her elbow. "Thanks Doc. I needed to hear that today. And thanks for lunch. I probably would have just grabbed an apple."

I shook my head. "Nope, no apples for you. Throw them all away right now."

"What? Why? What's wrong with apples?"

"An apple a day keeps the doctor away and I have no plans to stay away unless you adamantly tell me too, and even then, I'm not sure I could," I confessed.

Lucy burst out laughing.

"Was that supposed to be some weird pickup line or something? That was the worst joke ever."

I shrugged completely unaffected.

"Too cheesy?"

"Ridiculously cheesy."

There was a comfort settling in between us as we finished the meal, and I cleaned up our trash.

"Do you want to come inside?" she asked.

I looked down at my watch. "Unfortunately, no. Since I blew off most of yesterday it's been a busier than usual morning and my lunch break is nearly over. See you tomorrow?"

"Do I have a choice?" she teased.

"You always have a choice, Lucy."

I knew I'd said the right thing by the look on her face.

"In that case, I guess I'll see you tomorrow.

*****

It should have been my day off, but I got called in to deliver a baby. The labor took longer than expected and the little one was breech which required some maneuvering and prayers. At the end of it all I helped bring into this world a new little boy to welcome to the Pack.

I was exhausted and it was after six. I knew I should just call Lucy and apologize for not making it over. I had a good excuse for it, but my wolf was not happy with that decision, and I had to agree. I wanted, no I needed to see my mate.

I had a pot roast waiting for me in the crock pot and I had skipped lunch. I was starving. That posed a difficult decision: dinner or time with Lucy.

I sighed and picked up my phone dialing her number and I headed for home.

"Hello?" Lucy answered on the third ring. She sounded frazzled and it instantly set my wolf on edge.

"What's wrong?" I barked.

There was a moment of silence. "Micah?"

"Of course it's Micah. What's wrong?"

I was about to turn the car around and go straight to her, but she gave an exasperated sound.

"Nothing, and everything. It's fine, really. I'm afraid it's simply par for the course of a single mother. Vada is overly tired from her first week of school. I had tried to make it a low-key day to give her time to regroup, but she's just so cranky. I thought I would surprise her with a little fun and order pizza for dinner, but there's an hour backup."

"It is Saturday night."

"I realize that. I just hadn't thought it would be this busy or I would have ordered earlier."

"Does she like pot roast?" I blurted out just as I pulled up in front of my house.

"Uh, that's oddly specific, but yes. It's her absolute favorite actually and it's far too late to run to the store and get the ingredients, Micah. That's something that needs to cook all day."

"I'm on it. I'll be there in a few minutes."

I hung up the phone before she could tell me I was being ridiculous. I ran into the house, grabbed my crock pot and took it right back to the car. Then I drove over to Lucy's with a smile on my face surprised at just how great it made me feel to care for her.

I could certainly get used to it.

Parking and picking up our dinner, I took the front steps two at a time and knocked on Lucy's door.

"Mommy!" Vada yelled.

"I hear it," she mumbled seconds before the door opened.

There was a little girl with red rimmed eyes holding onto her leg for dear life.

"Mommy!" Vada yelled again. The young one looked up at me with huge eyes. She sniffed the air. "Food?"

"I'm told you like pot roast, Vada. Would you like to share my dinner?"

She abandoned her mother and toddled over to me.

"Doc," she said. "Eat."

I leaned down and swooped the girl up with one arm while balancing the pot in the other.

She giggled.

"Which way to the kitchen?"

Vada pointed and squealed happily.

Lucy

Chapter 7

I was on the verge of tears watching them.

Micah had Vada help him find three plates and silverware along with a serving spoon and set up the table. They both refused to let me help as they giggled and conspired while insisting I just sit and relax.

There was something sexy about a man with a baby in his arms. Plus, he was so nice to Vada. He had told me she wasn't the only lab baby he was acquainted with but seeing the way he treated her like a normal child made my heart melt and endeared him to me.

I had never truly had help with my daughter. It had always been just me and Vada. I had never dared to believe there could be anything else in the future, but as we sat down and ate the most incredible meal I could ever remember, my guard dropped where he was concerned.

"Mmm!" Vada exclaimed. "I yike. Doc, I yike."

"This really is delicious," I said. "Thank you. You really didn't have to do all of this. It's too much."

"Nonsense. I would have preferred to have spent the entire day spoiling you both. Typically, I would have had today off."

I didn't know how to feel about what he said. No one had ever spoiled me before. I knew I couldn't let him keep doing stuff like this, but for tonight, it had been sheer bliss to sit and let someone else handle the mundane daily needs such as making dinner.

"So where were you today, then?" I asked deciding not to comment on what he had said.

"I had a delivery. A baby. A baby boy to be specific. He was breech and the labor was long."

"And the baby is okay?" I inquired.

"Absolutely. I wouldn't be a very good doctor otherwise, now would I?"

"You can't help such a thing," I said with a frown.

"I know, and it happens rarely. I got lucky this time. No c-section necessary."

"I've only had to perform one. It was terrifying," I admitted.

He stared at me with a strange look on his face and I blushed. I couldn't believe I had mentioned that. Sure, he knew about Vada, and he'd done well with that, but he still didn't know all of my secrets and never could.

"You've executed a c-section before?"

"Yes. I've assisted with bringing dozens of babies into this world."

"So you're a midwife?"

"Not exactly. I just did what I had to do."

He considered that and nodded. I knew that he had privilege to more information about what happened inside the Raglan compounds than the average person, but I wasn't certain just how much he knew.

"Maybe you should be," he said casually before popping a potato into his mouth.

"Should be what?"

"A midwife."

I had never considered such a thing before.

"I haven't thought of that. I do have to get a job and soon or we won't be able to afford to stay here. I was supposed to be job hunting this week, but nothing has gone as planned. Every day it's been something or another."

"Well, what sort of thing are you looking for?"

"Literally anything."

He looked like he was on the verge of wolfing out when I mentioned I might not be able to afford to stay. Kyle Westin was being very gracious in helping us out, but it wasn't right, and I needed to be able to pull my own weight and stand on my own two feet. Vada counted on me, and I couldn't let her down.

"I've worked a few waitressing jobs, and some retail, but I really don't have much in the way of professional experience after, well, you know."

I thought maybe if I kept talking, he'd calm down some.

"It hasn't been a year yet," he said between clenched teeth.

"Huh?"

"Westin Pack took a vote to support every shifter the Raglan held that needed it for one year. We all agreed to a decreased stipend for that time to ensure none of you had to go without or struggle as you started your new life. Why aren't you getting your cut to help with this stuff?"

I sighed. "Kyle's allowing us to stay here rent free. Anything more was too much." I had lost everything. Vada and what was left of my dignity was all I had left in the world and my pride wouldn't let me take a handout. I could do this on my own. I hated not paying my way, and in some weird way, it made me feel indebted, or even enslaved to Kyle, just for the small bit I had accepted.

"Lucy, this program is supposed to help. We're all pitching in for this, every single Westin wolf."

"I don't want to be indebted to you," I blurted out.

I could see the hurt on his face and knowing I'd caused it cut me right through the heart.

"I didn't mean you specifically," I said quietly.

"Are you sure about that?" I asked.

Vada toddled back into the room and climbed up into his lap as if it were the most natural thing in the world.

"Tired. Doc. Sleep?"

He looked a little confused.

"Come on pumpkin, I'll put you to bed," I said standing up to reach for her.

She shook her little head. "Doc. Sleep."

"Honey, he's our guest. He doesn't need to put you to bed."

He frowned at me. "What is mommy talking about? I would be honored to put you to bed."

I stared at him like he was crazy. Vada was not the easiest kid to put down. She knew when she was tired and that she wanted to go to bed, but she would insist on brushing her teeth and then her hair. She would request five books read to her, three glasses of water, only one of which I would agree to, a minimum of two trips to the bathroom, and a bedtime snack which she knew she wouldn't get because she'd already brushed her teeth, but we'd negotiate on a small treat with breakfast the next morning instead. It could be a trying ordeal.

Vada giggled, jumped down from his lap as her tiny hand wrapped around his finger.

"I show you."

She dragged him through the house to her room, but not before stopping at the bathroom to brush her teeth and pull out her hairbrush.

I stood back and just watched him. I had no idea why I was even allowing it. I really didn't know how long I'd be able to afford staying here and the last thing I needed was for Vada to get too attached to him. It would only hurt more when we moved on.

Still, I couldn't bring myself to stop them as I watched in fascination as she told him how to brush her hair and then tried to take him to her room no doubt for her first book.

"Nope. Potty first, big girl."

"No, Doc."

"Yes, Vada. You just finished dinner and it's time for bed. You need to use the potty first like all big girls have to do."

"Big girl?"

"Yes, you."

"I a big girl."

"Yes, you are. And big girls go potty before bed."

She sighed dramatically and then much to my shock she went to the bathroom for him. Micah turned his back to her to give her privacy and winked at me when he saw me watching them.

I blushed feeling like I had just been caught.

"All done," Vada said grabbing his finger once more. "Book, Doc."

"Not yet, big girl. We have to wash hands first."

She frowned at him. "Book."

"Proper hygiene. Wash those little hands, cutie pie."

"Doc, too?"

"Doc too," he agreed as they washed their hands together as Vada giggled at the funny faces he made.

This time, he scooped her up in his arms and threw her over his shoulder as she shrieked in delight.

"Where to?"

"My room."

"This one?" he asked opening the door to the linen closet.

"No, silly."

"How about this one?" he asked opening my door at the end of the hall.

"Dat mommy's room."

"Oh, mommy's room? Then where is Vada's room?"

"Dare, right dare, Doc."

"This one?" he asked walking into her room.

"Yes!"

They both cheered. I didn't have the heart to tell him he was only winding her up, making it far harder to actually get her to sleep.

"Book," she demanded.

"One book, then bed."

"No, Doc. Five."

He chuckled. "Two, and that's my final offer."

She pouted. "Two."

He sat down in the rocking chair in the corner of her room as she picked out only two books. Then she climbed up and settled onto his lap.

He started to read. His voice was so soothing. I sat down in the hall outside her room and just listened. Much to my surprise I started to dose off.

"Lucy?" Micah said.

I hadn't even made it to the end of the book.

"How many did she make you read?"

He chuckled. "She didn't even make it through one and neither did you."

"Only one? She usually demands five."

"She tried."

I yawned.

"Looks like it's time for you to call it a night too."

The next thing I knew strong arms wrapped around me as he lifted me into his warm embrace and carried me down the hall to my room.

He pulled the covers back and carefully laid me down then tucked me in as if I were the most precious thing in the world.

I wanted to tell him to stay, but I really was exhausted. It had been such a long day and my eyes suddenly didn't want to stay open a moment longer.

He leaned down and kissed my forehead.

"Sweet dreams. I'll let myself out."

*****

The next morning, I awoke with a jolt. The sun was streaming in and as I listened to the silence around me there was no sign of Vada.

I launched myself out of bed and ran into her room where I found my daughter still asleep.

I checked the time to find it was after nine. I couldn't remember the last time she had slept this long. Had she ever?

I walked out to the kitchen to make some coffee. I needed it.

I had expected to find the dirty dishes from dinner still sitting on the table, but they weren't there. In fact, the entire kitchen had been scrubbed clean. I walked into the living room and Vada's toys had all been picked up and neatly put away.

It felt as if I had awoken to some sort of alternate universe. This was most definitely not my life.

I headed back to the kitchen and called Micah while I attempted to make coffee only then realizing I was out of filters.

"Did you do this?" I asked the second the phone connected. "Because if not, then I'm probably going to freak out."

"Well, good morning to you too."

"Did you do this?"

"Do what, Luce?"

No one ever called me that, but it made me feel all warm and fuzzy to hear the shortened version of my name on his lips.

"Lucy? You still there?"

"Oh, yeah, sorry. My house is clean. I know it wasn't when I went to bed."

"It was nothing. I just straightened up a little. I guess I have a bit of a nightly routine too."

"I cannot stand waking up to a sink full of dirty dishes," I blurted out. "You couldn't possibly know that about me, but it's true, so thank you."

I could hear the smile on his face. "You're welcome, and I too can't stand to wake to a dirty or unkempt house. Everything was already tidy, there were just a few toys and our dishes from dinner. It was no big deal."

"It was to me," I whispered.

"It was the least I could do for you letting me crash your evening."

I snorted. "Really? You brought dinner to us. You put Vada to bed in record time, and then me too." I wanted to ask why he hadn't tried to stay the night, but I bit my tongue. "And seriously, what did you do to my daughter? Did you drug her or something Doc?" I teased.

"What? No. I would never."

I laughed. "I was only teasing you. I know you would never hurt her, or me."

It was true too. My brain said I shouldn't let him in, but my heart overrode that. I trusted him completely.

"I'm glad she's giving you a break. And I'm glad you called. It took a lot not to just show back up with a cup of hot coffee and beg you to let me stay."

Micah

Chapter 8

I had just laid my cards out on the table and waited with bated breath for her to respond.

"I certainly wouldn't have minded that this morning. I'm out of coffee filters," she said with a yawn.

I grinned to myself. "I'm on my way."

I was still lying in bed naked and hard from thinking of her. I was just about to take care of that when Lucy called. Seeing her would be even better.

I quickly put on a fresh pot of coffee unsure of how she took it but figured she'd have what she needed at her house anyway. While it was brewing, I got dressed, and filled a large thermos, grabbed half a pack of filters and made my way to Lucy's house as quickly as possible.

I was just about to knock on the door when I heard a scream followed by a loud bang. I practically knocked the door off its hinges as I burst into the room. My wolf was on edge but was going into a fury when I smelled blood.

"Lucy? Lucy, where are you?"

"Dammit. We're back here."

I could barely hear anything over the roaring in my ears, but as I walked down the hall still clenching the thermos that probably had claw prints in it, I could hear Vada's sobs.

"Is everything okay?"

"Fine," she said but I could feel her anxiety rising. Something was going on and she clearly didn't want me to know about it. "You're practically wolfing out. We're okay."

She surprised me by reaching out and touching my arm. It calmed my wolf in an instant.

"What happened?"

"It was nothing, really, just a minor accident."

Vada's eyes were puffy and red, and the shower curtain was pulled off the wall. I knew I had smelled blood but there only seemed to be a tiny amount on the floor next to a razor. I leaned down and picked it up as the little girl withdrew from it.

I didn't say a word but put it up high and out of her reach in the shower.

"I can fix this."

"It's okay," she insisted. "I'll get it later."

Why was she so nervous? It looked like a normal casual accident.

"I falled," Vada confessed. "Owie, Doc."

"Well, I can fix that all up. Where does it hurt?"

She pointed to her leg where there was a very faint red line.

"Well, it looks okay. Not too bad."

"Mommy fix. All better."

"Mommy's are good at making everything better, huh?"

Her head bobbed up and down.

I smiled, but when I turned to look at Lucy her face was drained of color, and I thought she might be sick. Our bond was beginning to grow which thrilled me, but in that moment, it also terrified me, because whatever had happened in there before I arrived had Lucy scared, really scared.

I set down the thermos and filters and pulled her into my arms.

"Hey, she's okay. Everything's okay."

I held her closely until she started to calm down.

"Hungry!" Vada yelled. "I hungry."

I snatched her up with one arm while Lucy reached for the coffee and Ziploc bag of filters I'd brought.

"What is this?" she asked.

I shrugged, never taking my arm from around her as the three of us walked to the kitchen as one.

"You mentioned you were out. I just bought a pack. Should last you a few weeks at least."

She looked up at me with confusion and happiness shining through her eyes. I was trying not to read too much into it.

I smirked. "I mean, I can just bring coffee by every morning if you prefer."

She shook her head, but there was a smile on her lips.

I stared at her lips for longer than I should have not willing to let her go just yet. I wanted to kiss her so badly, but I sensed she wasn't ready. If it were left up to me, we'd already have sealed the bond growing between us.

I had nearly lost it when I discovered she was my true mate and thought she'd already taken another mate. Once I learned she hadn't, then as far as I was concerned, she was mine… period, end of story.

"Ew, stinky," Vada protested squirming in my grasp. "Doc, pooted."

"No, I didn't."

"Stinky poot." She was waving her hand in front of her nose.

I sniffed the air. "I don't smell anything."

Lucy sniffed and her eyes went wide then she gave me a stern look and yanked Vada from my hold.

"What? I swear I didn't."

"I know, but you are scenting."

"I am?"

"You're a doctor, of shifters. You should know when you're scenting."

"I've never done it before. I don't even know how. I've only studied it clinically. How can you even tell?"

Lucy blushed furiously.

"Lucy?" I asked.

"Because to me it smells good," she blurted out. "And clearly, to Vada it does not."

We stared at each other for a moment and then right when it should have turned awkward, we both burst out laughing.

"I'm sorry, Vada."

Lucy motioned for me to sit while she buzzed around the kitchen. Two coffee mugs, a bowl, a box of cereal, and a sippy cup of milk later she finally sat, poured the coffee and passed me one of the mugs.

I made a mental note that she drank her coffee black. It was the tiny details that I wanted to document as I got to know her. So far everything about Lucy was perfect, maybe even a little too perfect. I couldn't find a single fault with her. I wasn't sure if that was the bond or just her.

If I had any complaint at all it was that she was extremely independent. I didn't think she realized I was trying to help her. If I had come right out and said "let me bring dinner over" she probably would have told me no last night, but in a moment where her defenses were down, I was able to sneak in and care for her without setting off any alarms. This morning had been much the same.

Vada ate quietly while Lucy and I sipped our coffee. It dawned on me that it was the most peaceful and perfect morning I'd had in years.

For the first time in my entire life, I knew this was exactly where I was supposed to be.

"Thank you for this," Lucy finally said.

I nodded. "Anytime."

*****

Sunday had been comfortable and perfect as I got to hang out with my two favorite girls. We'd watched TV, played outside, and Lucy had snuggled up against me as we talked and got to know each other better while Vada took her afternoon nap.

I'd treated them both to the pizza they had missed out on the night before.

It was pretty close to perfect.

With each passing day I could feel our bond strengthening and I knew Lucy was growing comfortable with me. It took a lot of willpower not to kiss her and touch her the way I longed too, but I knew she had been through quite the ordeal and baby steps would be best for my long-term chances. I was terrified of scaring her off by jumping too soon.

When Monday arrived, life blurred quickly. I managed a thirty-minute break between appointments when I shifted and literally ran to Lucy's house. I had thought ahead enough to carry my clothes with me, but she must have sensed me coming because she walked out onto her back porch as if she were looking for me. Of course, she busted me mid-shift.

I had froze as I stood there naked before her. We were shifters and nudity wasn't a big deal, but we were also newly mating and that affected things. When I smelled her arousal at the sight of me, certain parts had sprung to life right before her very eyes.

There was no way I could have controlled it.

She had gasped and averted her eyes. I was tempted not to dress after that and see how far things would go, but I also knew I had to get back to work quickly so I had dressed and essentially cock blocked myself.

Much to my surprise, she'd made soup and it was waiting for me. She'd denied it when I challenged her on that fact, but she'd blushed instantly giving herself away.

Knowing she had been hoping I'd stop by made me deliriously happy.

"Will you be coming by tonight?"

"Do you want me to?"

She shrugged. "You're welcome to, but we're having the same thing for dinner."

"It's delicious, but I have appointments booked through nine tonight."

"That late?" she asked sounding disappointed. "But won't you get a break for dinner at least?"

"Nope. Afraid not. I keep snacks at the office for days like this, but otherwise this will probably be the only thing I eat today."

"Did you skip breakfast too?"

I shrugged. "Not the coffee."

She scowled and shook her head. "I'll swing by and drop some soup off on my way to pick up Vada. If you're running back in your fur there's no way you can carry it with you now."

I started to tell her she didn't have to, but then bit my tongue.

"Okay, that would be great."

It was hard to walk away from her, but I knew I had patients waiting for me. Still, I took my time undressing on her back porch. She was inside, but I could see her shadow through the window just as I had that first time I'd gone for a run and my wolf had taken me right to her backyard.

*****

The afternoon dragged on. One patient after another. It had been this way for months, mostly those displaced after the big rescue. They were rarely sick or even injured. It felt like I played the role of psychiatrist more than physician lately.

When my two o'clock finally left at a quarter to three, I was feeling exasperated and more than ready for a break.

The bell out front chimed again. I hated that damn bell. I wanted to throw it out the window.

I took a moment to regain my composure and then walked out to the front lobby.

My entire demeanor changed as I stepped closer. I could smell Lucy.

By the time she saw me I was grinning from ear to ear.

"You came."

"I told you I would."

I hugged her like it was the most natural thing in the world and I kissed the top of her head before letting go.

"Perfect timing. I'm starving."

"Are you free?"

I looked down at my watch. "Nope, less than ten minutes until my next patient arrives."

"You better eat quickly then."

I shrugged. "I'd rather spend it with you and warm it up later. Thanks for bringing it by."

"Can I ask you something? Where is your receptionist?"

I laughed. "No such luck. Actually, with the increase in patient activity lately, I was just approved to hire on some help."

"Approved? You need approval for that?"

"No, but if I want Kyle to pay the wages instead of it coming out of my pocket then I do."

"Smart. So what are you looking for?"

"Just an admin really, though someone with medical training would be a huge plus to offset a little of the workload. Why, you interested?"

"Yes," she blurted out and then I saw it register on her face after the fact like there was a delay between her quick response and the info actually reaching her brain.

"Really?"

"I don't know if it would be a good idea, but I really need a job."

I considered it for a moment. Could I handle working with Lucy all day every day? Yes, yes I could. My wolf practically howled at the thought.

Still, I had to think about what's best for her.

"There are other places hiring, like I know Jesse down at The Crate is looking for a waitress."

"I saw the sign today and almost applied."

"What stopped you?"

"He's probably going to want me to work the evening shift at least some of the time and then what do I do with Vada? There are so many other things to consider and ensure she's cared for first and foremost."

I loved how fiercely protective of her child she was.

"You can always leave Vada with me," I offered.

After I opened my big mouth I considered what I'd just said and yes, I would be fine with it too. I knew they came as a pair. Lucy was mine, therefore, Vada was too. It was the first time I had let myself think of her in that way.

I took a breath expecting to have a sudden freak out, but it didn't come. I didn't just want to be a mate to Lucy, but also a father to Vada. I had always loved kids and I was ready for this.

"That's sweet, but it could be a regular thing and you have so much else to do."

"Well, you said you had midwife experience. Anything else?" I asked her, surprising myself that I was actually considering this.

She bit her lip, and I could feel she was still holding something back from me.

"Nothing formal, but I aided and assisted hundreds during captivity. The Raglan would have just left them to die without a care so there were a few of us that pitched in to help whenever possible."

"Okay, but most of the job will likely be boring, answering phones, setting up appointments, organizing and pulling patient files, stuff like that. Are you sure you want that?"

"I know you sometimes work late, like tonight. I would have to pick Vada up from school and bring her back here on those nights."

"I mean, you two are always welcome here. I don't mind her hanging out here at all. There's even a spare room that we can turn into a safe playroom for her even, but are you sure you're okay with this?"

"This? What?"

"Working every day, with me."

I needed her to say yes. It suddenly felt like the most important moment of my life as I waited.

She smirked. "That's not exactly a hardship."

"It's not?"

She gave me a weird look and shook her head as I felt like my heart was about to explode in my chest. It was the first true sign of acceptance I have felt from her. Sure, there had been smaller things, but this felt major.

"To be honest, I think my wolf would be a lot happier and more settled if I were close to you each day."

I couldn't stop myself this time. I wasn't going to hold back. I closed the gap between us, and I kissed her as if my life depended on it.

She gasped and then sighed as she kissed me back.

Lucy

Chapter 9

I vaguely remembered hearing the little bell chime as the door opened behind me.

Micah pulled back abruptly cutting our kiss off.

"Nonna. I'll be with you in just a moment."

"Woo wee, if that's the kind of treatments you're handing out these days, sign me up, lover boy."

The tips of Micah's ears actually darkened.

"Sorry," he whispered to me. "That's my three o'clock."

My head was still in a daze, until I heard three o'clock.

"Wait, it's three?"

"Yeah, or about. She usually arrives a few minutes early."

"I have to pick up Vada," I practically shouted.

He stilled me with his touch. "Hey, we'll talk more tonight about… you know," he said glancing over at Nonna.

I was well aware of who she was and had already suspected she was a bit of a gossip around town. Making out with the Pack physician in between appointments was not exactly the thing I wanted everyone in Westin Pack to know about me.

"We're cool?"

"Yes, but I really have to run. And don't forget to eat," I yelled over my shoulder as I ran out of the building transitioning fully into mom mode.

I could hear Micah chuckling as the door closed behind me.

I raced over to the school. There were still cars lined up, but I was the last of the line. I usually parked and went inside, but as soon as Vanessa saw me, she disappeared and returned with Vada.

"Hi Mommy."

"Hi pumpkin. Did you have a good day?" I turned to Vanessa before Vada could respond. "I'm really sorry. I was running behind."

I certainly wasn't going to tell her that I was making out with Micah and lost track of time. I knew my cheeks were burning just thinking about it.

"Lucy, you're fine. We had a great day today, didn't we?" she asked my daughter who smiled brightly and nodded. "See you tomorrow, Vada."

"Bye, Nessa."

I knew I had to stop thinking of him and concentrate on my little girl in the back seat.

When we pulled up to the house, there was a car waiting out front. I knew it wasn't Micah's. I didn't recognize it at all.

The door opened as I parked, and I got out and walked around to put myself between the newcomer and Vada.

A very large man stepped out of the driver's seat.

He nodded at me. "Lucy."

I would never forget that face and those eyes of steel.

"Silas?"

He smiled at me, though somehow it didn't soften his glare any.

The passenger door of the car opened and closed.

"I heard a rumor you were here." Vada, the woman who had saved me countless times, had delivered my daughter into this world, and who I cherished so much that I'd named my kid after her, stepped from the car.

In seconds I was wrapped in her embrace as I was consumed by emotions.

"Vada?"

"I here, Mommy," my daughter said.

I laughed through tears.

The elder Vada let go of me as I turned to help my daughter out of her car seat. I lifted her into my arms.

"Sweetheart, this is Vada, too."

"Hi," she said shyly.

"Hi, Vada. Can I hold you?"

My little girl shot me a look, but I smiled and nodded.

Vada took her from me. I watched the two of them together as little Vada sniffed her shoulder and then pulled back.

"I know you."

"I know you, too. Silas, isn't she the most precious thing in the world?"

The man that I was certain was made of ice literally melted as he watched them.

I took a moment to really look at them and my jaw dropped.

"You're having a baby?"

Vada practically beamed. "We are."

"She's not due until Spring," Silas informed me.

I reached out and touched her round protruding belly.

"Are you sure?"

"We're sure. Though Doc believes it to be twins."

"How wonderful."

"If you're truly sticking around here, Lucy, I would love for you to be there to assist with my delivery."

Silas stiffened and I could see how protective he was of her. I had to assume he was her mate. I vaguely remember hearing they were mating when I last saw her during the big rescue.

"I yike Doc," my little one announced cutting through the tension Silas was experiencing.

I could be crazy, but it felt like maybe all Vadas had a bit of magic over that man.

"We are just getting home from school, but I have soup simmering. I know it's a little early, but would you both like to stay for dinner?"

Vada hesitated and Silas looked back towards the car.

"We have friends with us, Tarron and Susan. I know it was a crazy day the last we saw each other, but both Silas and Tarron are part of Westin Force and were there for the rescue."

"Well then, I'd love to thank him too. There's plenty for everyone."

Silas nodded towards the car and the two strangers stepped out.

"Hi, I'm Susan," the woman said.

There was something about her that I instantly liked.

"Welcome, come on in."

Normally I didn't like people in my space. It stressed my wolf out, but for some reason, and I suspected it had a lot to do with a certain doctor, she was feeling extremely agreeable.

The next few hours we talked and laughed. I had the best time with them as they all doted on my daughter as she ran around or sat and played nearby.

My first impressions were rarely wrong, and this was no exception. I truly liked Susan.

"So," she said biting her lower lip. "Vada tells me you like playing games," Susan finally blurted out.

"I remember you always playing with the others."

I shrugged. "There wasn't exactly much else to do. Even when we were caged, we could still play or at least pretend to play Dungeon's and Dragons. Of course we didn't have the proper tools and dice and all to really play, but we made up ways around that and made it work. The story telling alone provided a great escape for many of us."

"You play D&D?" Tarron asked.

"Not for a long time. I don't even know if I'd remember how."

"Oh please, once you're in, you're in for life. It's like riding a bicycle, just comes back to you."

"Do you play?" I asked him.

"Hell yes. Every Wednesday night. You should come."

"I just went for the first time last week. Tarron's been begging me to give it a try. I'll admit, it was a lot more fun than I expected. You're welcome to join us this week. We play from six to eight."

I considered it for a minute, but that wasn't the type of thing I could just bring Vada too.

"It sounds fun, but…"

"But nothing. You're in," Tarron said.

I shook my head. "I don't have anyone to watch Vada and I wouldn't really enjoy it if I was worried about keeping an eye on her too. I doubt kids tag along to those things."

"Oh, let me babysit," Vada said. "Please, Lucy. Silas and I can care for her on Wednesday nights while you take a break doing something you enjoy. It would be doing us both a huge favor."

"How would pawning off my kid help you?" I laughed.

"Well, neither of us really expected to have kids. Okay, we don't know anything about babies," she confessed.

"Not a damn thing," Silas confirmed.

"I've been studying though, and we babysat for Shelby's triplets once."

Her eyes had a faraway glaze over them as if she was remembering a nightmare.

"No one died," Silas confessed.

Vada elbowed him. "It wasn't that bad, but three at once was a bit terrifying."

"Three at once would terrify me and I've had two years of on-the-job training for this."

The others chuckled.

"So, what do you say?"

"Come on, say yes, please," Susan practically begged.

"You heard the big guy. No one died on their watch," Tarron teased.

They were all staring and waiting for me to respond.

"Okay," I finally agreed. "But on a week-by-week trial basis. If it goes bad this week, then it's over."

"Fair enough," Vada said with a squeal of excitement.

She looked up at Silas as he grinned and gave her a quick kiss.

Tarron had his arm around Susan as she rested her head on his shoulder.

The sight of the couples gave me a weird empty feeling.

I wished my mate was there with us, too.

My mate? When had I let myself acknowledge Micah as my mate?

The thought was starting to make me freak out a little. I needed a mental subject change and quick.

"Who's ready for dinner?"

Micah

Chapter 10

If Monday was crazy, Tuesday was sheer insanity.

I didn't have a moment of free time until I collapsed into bed at ten o'clock. I stared at the clock debating on whether I should call her or not. In the end, my need to just hear my mate's voice overruled the possibility of her already being asleep.

"Hey, is everything okay?" she asked when she answered.

"No. I didn't get to see you today, but at least I get to hear your voice before I pass out."

"I missed you too," she confessed. "Is every day like this for you?"

"No. I do try to take time off too. I mean a birth, accident, or unexpected illness will screw with that. I am on-call twenty-four hours a day, but it's rare really."

"How's tomorrow looking?" she asked.

I smiled. "I take Wednesdays off."

"Really?"

"Really."

"I drop Vada off at school at eight. Want to come by after that?"

It was the first time she had initiated an invitation to me. So far it had mostly been me taking advantage of moments and openings that arose on the fly. She had offered to bring me dinner the night before. That had been Lucy's idea not mine, but since I was the one benefiting from it, it hadn't felt like her initiating it. This time it was different. She was inviting me into her space.

"I would love that. I do have plans in the afternoon and throughout the evening. I'm sorry. It's sort of a standing thing each week."

"It's fine. I have plans tomorrow evening too."

"You do?"

"Yup."

I grinned imagining various things she and Vada were likely going to be up to. I almost wished it wasn't D&D night so I could join them. I knew I couldn't do that to my players though. Wednesdays meant too much to me to give it up now.

"See you tomorrow then?" she asked hopefully.

"Wouldn't miss it for the world. Sweet dreams, Lucy."

"Sweet dreams, Micah."

*****

I was on her front steps waiting for her to get home from dropping Vada off at school. I had barely slept, excited to just spend some time alone with my mate.

"You're early," she said with a happy smile.

I shrugged. "Couldn't wait."

I walked to her and pulled her into my arms kissing her for the whole world to see. We'd been interrupted the last time and I'd certainly heard about it for the duration of Nonna's visit. I hadn't considered she would know Lucy already, but apparently the old lady had taken an instant liking to her and since she had been the one to give Lucy directions to my office the day she'd brought Vada in, Nonna now attributed our pairing to her own match making skills.

None of that was on my mind though as my lips brushed Lucy's.

I didn't know what to expect or how she would react. I knew I had taken her by surprise in my office, but she wasn't shy or holding back as she kissed me.

Her hands fisted in my hair, and she pulled me down closer until I felt as if we were fused as one.

My body was on fire, and I was ready to take her right there and mark her mine forever. I had just enough sense left in my brain to hold back from making that happen. We hadn't discussed long term yet and I wouldn't force myself on her.

I did however reach down and enjoy the feel of the curve of her ass in my hands. She fit to me perfectly. I lifted her easily and she wrapped her legs around my waist bringing us intimately close.

Our lips never parted as I carried her into the house and sat down on the couch so she was straddling me.

I didn't even try to take things to the next level, just enjoyed making out with my girl all morning until we were both starving and had to break for lunch.

Lucy kept looking at me and blushing as she cooked hamburgers for us to eat. I would never turn down good food, or just sitting back and watching my mate as she moved around the kitchen, though I was quite certain I would happily starve to death just feasting on her for the rest of my life.

My head was swimming with passion and my heart light. My wolf was even unusually quiet where I had expected him to be aggressively pushing for me to mark her.

For just a moment, I let myself believe this was my life.

With the burgers ready, she finally sat down across from me and pulled her knees up to her chest. I was good at reading people, and I knew it was an external sign that she was trying to protect herself, yet she kept looking up at me and grinning.

"Are you sure you're really up for working with me every single day?" I teased but also wondering how in the hell I was going to keep my hands off of her now that I'd had a taste of her sweet lips.

"I don't know if it would be a good idea, but I do really need a job."

"Can you start tomorrow?" I surprised us both by asking. "I would have given you the grand tour and walked through everything today, but I think I had better uses of my day off this morning."

She blushed again, but still couldn't hide the grin.

"We're going to need some ground rules," she insisted. "Like no messing around in the office."

"I can't promise that. How about no messing around in the office in front of patients?"

"I think you already broke that one, boss."

I gave her a funny look and then burst out laughing. I certainly hadn't expected her to make light of the situation so quickly.

"Fair enough, but I'll try."

"What are my hours and what's the pay? If we're being serious about this, these are important questions."

"Fine. What time does Vada get dropped off and picked up?"

She rolled her eyes. "You can't make my schedule around Vada's. This is business."

"To hell I can't. I can set whatever hours I like. It's eight to three, right?"

"If you already knew the answer, why are you asking?"

"Just making sure I had that right."

"Eight to three."

"Okay, so the clinic opens at nine on Monday, Tuesday, Thursday, and Friday. In general I close at five, but as you already know, that rarely happens. Still, if we can do eight-thirty to five, taking lunch from twelve to one and then a thirty minute Vada break around three, we're good."

I could see her mentally counting up the hours in her head.

"That's only seven hours four days a week, only part time."

"I'm paying $35 an hour."

She considered that. "Okay, but are you sure? That's way overpriced for a receptionist."

"With medical experience," I added, careful not to say medically trained. "Plus, there will be additional things I could use assistance with and the days off aren't a guarantee."

"For the most part, that's okay with me. I will need time to find a sitter for Vada in the evenings."

"No, Vada will come to work with us. I'll get one of the storage rooms cleaned out this weekend to give her a safe room to play in when times get busy. For this she can just hang out in the front area with you while I'm with patients. It's not that big of a deal unless it becomes problematic for you. Or if you'd rather, I could talk to Emma and see if she'd be interested in working a few evening hours. Bravo team is home right now so unless something happens, she may prefer to spend her time with her mate. She's a gorilla shifter, but she's fantastic with kids. She watches Shelby and Ben's triplets during school hours. Shelby's a teacher."

She nodded. "I know who they are. I've been trying to work up the nerve to reach out to her."

"You should do that."

By the time she agreed on my terms of employment, it was sadly time to say goodbye. I knew the boys would forgive me if I bailed on them, but I didn't want to be the guy who let down his friends at the last second either.

With another kiss, I left her with plans to see her in the morning.

*****

"What has gotten into you?" Baine demanded. "Last week you couldn't play for shit and today you're on fire."

"Went for a run, didn't you?" Grant asked as I watched the ball sail out of my hands and right through the hoop for a perfect net ball.

"I did actually. Thanks for that. It was rather life changing."

"Life changing? What kind of bullshit are you spouting off now, Doc?" Baine challenged.

I laughed. "Well, can you fools just shut up and play the game already? I swear you're bigger gossips than Nonna."

"Hey now, no one is a bigger gossip than that," Tarron pointed out making us all laugh. There was no doubt just how much that man loved the crazy old woman who insisted on adopting him, the lone fox shifter at the time, and then take in all of his mate's sisters claiming them as her own.

My heart wasn't really in the game. I was rather kicking myself for not taking things to the next level with Lucy while we would have been truly uninterrupted.

I hadn't told her what I had going on today or how I played basketball with Bravo team every Wednesday then spent the evening geeking out over Dungeons and Dragons. I liked to think she saw me as a rather cool guy. Would that change her impression of me?

I knew I couldn't let that worry me. She'd find out eventually and would have to come to accept it. I was too invested to just quit now. I would do anything for my mate, but that might be testing my limits.

*****

I was hosting tonight. I had snacks lining the island counter and a big pot of chili waiting for my guests. Susan had apparently enjoyed playing with us and Tarron had told me she was coming again and this time she was bringing a friend.

I always loved introducing new people to the game.

Of course, they were the last to arrive.

"Wow, something smells good in here."

I shook my head unable to believe my ears.

Tarron and Susan walked in. I saw Susan sniff the air and then shrug.

"I don't really smell anything."

"Really?"

I was on my feet and crossing the room before Lucy even came into view.

She came to an abrupt stop when she saw me. "Micah? What are you doing here?"

"It's his house," Tarron informed her eyeballing me suspiciously.

"Hey," I told her wrapping her up in my arms and kissing her to make it absolutely clear that this girl was mine.

"What the hell? Is this why you were practically dancing out of your skin all afternoon?"

I raised my middle finger to him.

Tarron shook his head. "Promises, promises. Wait until the guys hear about this."

"You didn't tell me you were mating," Susan said to Lucy.

I realized she was a bit embarrassed having just been put on the spot and maybe even by my aggressive move to claim her.

"It's not really something people talk about, is it?"

"Oh, we definitely talk about it." Susan linked arms with Lucy and dragged her away from me and over to the table. "This Friday night is ladies' night. You're coming. I don't want to hear any excuses. Trust me, you need this."

"I can't. I'm not asking Vada to watch my kid again this week. I'm not even confident they'll survive tonight," she said.

"Vada and Silas are babysitting?" I asked and I could see concern on her face.

"They really do need the practice," Susan confessed.

"But not on her," I argued in disbelief. I could feel my wolf perk up and listen in. He wasn't any happier about this than I was.

"They're fine," Tarron argued. "But if you're so worried about it, then you watch the kid Friday night."

"Okay," I said without a second thought.

"Okay?" Lucy asked, sounding surprised.

That didn't sit well with me. Vada was mine too. Of course I would watch her.

"Yes, go enjoy ladies' night. I'll watch the baby. Done. Now, can we get this game started?"

Lucy laughed but she didn't argue with me. "You're the DM?"

"Of course I am."

I had no idea how Susan had convinced her to come tonight. It obviously had nothing to do with me because Lucy had been genuinely shocked to see me. I didn't care if she knew anything at all about the game. If she was willing to just hang out and learn, I would be thrilled to teach her. It was more than I could have ever hoped for.

I loved Dungeons and Dragons almost as much as I loved her.

I stared at her for a minute. I loved Lucy. There was no doubt in my mind. I loved caring for her and making her laugh. I loved spending time with her. Just hearing her voice last night had righted my bad day. I was in love with my mate, and I quickly learned that she was in love with D&D, too.

She was good, really good. I mean I knew she was intelligent and quick witted, but damn. I was turned on more than ever watching her play and strategize throughout the night.

When everyone finally said good night, she pulled me to the side.

"Are you serious about babysitting Friday night?"

"Are you seriously okay with that?"

She nodded. "I've been a little edgy tonight and I'm anxious to get back and check on Vada. Silas just texts me updates of 'no one's dead' which really isn't helping to calm my nerves."

I laughed and shook my head. "He certainly has a way about him. It's an acquired taste though."

"I can see that. I would actually feel a lot better if you were with her."

She looked both hopeful and nervous.

"I'll be there," I said leaning down to give her a quick kiss. I knew I couldn't deepen it no matter how much I wanted to. She needed to get back to Vada and Susan and Tarron were waiting in the car to take her home.

"Do you think I should do this?"

"I think it would be good for you. They are a crazy, but great group of ladies."

"You know them?"

I laughed. "Luce, I know everyone around here."

"Right. So I should do this?"

"Yes. And Vada and I will be fine."

"I know," she said confidently.

"Plus, it will be good for you to make friends and start finding your place around here."

I had already said too much, but I needed that more than anything. Because I knew the more she settled in San Marco, the better my odds were that she would stay. I needed her to stay because I couldn't imagine not having her in my life.

Thoughts of her leaving scared the shit out of me.

Lucy

Chapter 11

I was excited to start my new job, but nervous about working so closely with Micah. I knew I was getting too close and enjoying his kisses a little too much. He made me feel things I'd never experienced before and certainly had me thinking things that were not appropriate for work.

I had no idea how I was going to manage to keep the two separated.

My first day started off great. He gave me a tour around the place, showed me the files, which to my surprise were all offline and old school paper files.

"Why don't you have these scanned into a computer or something? Wouldn't it be much easier to find patient information that way?"

Micah laughed. "Yeah, it would definitely be easier, but my father and his father before him did it this way and quite frankly, I haven't had time to do anything about it. I came back here and basically hit the ground running straight out of med school."

I made a mental note to research types of programs and security for such things. I had no idea what I was getting myself into, but what would it hurt to at least look into options for him?

Much to my surprise after the way he had kissed me in front of everyone at the D&D game, Micah was the epitome of professional. It was frustrating me more than anything. How could he be so calm and collected, completely unaffected by my presence here when I was going insane with desire just being this close for so long and not touching him.

Of course, there had been the occasional brushes in passing and while he was giving me the tour of the place, but that was it. And it was hardly enough to even begin to calm my wolf, or my libido.

At five minutes to noon, Micah walked out his latest patient and then locked the doors behind him. He turned to me and clapped his hands together. “Hungry? I’m starved. Finish up whatever you’re doing or stop when you get to a break point and come on back to my office.”

He turned and walked away.

I stared at him somewhat stunned by his behavior. It was true I had asked him to stay professional and keep his hands to himself during business hours, but I didn’t think he’d take it to this extreme. My body was practically buzzing being so near him. Why wasn’t he going just as insane by my presence?

I finished what I was doing and walked to his office. I peeked in, but he wasn’t at his desk.

I yelped when a hand snaked out and grabbed me around the waist, pulling me into the room, and closing the door behind us.

“Finally,” Micah sighed seconds before his lips pressed against mine.

He had me pinned up against the wall and his mouth was claiming me.

I moaned, letting the emotions consume me as his demanding kisses stoked a flame deep within me.

I needed him.

I had never needed anyone as badly as I needed Micah.

He eased up a little, talking as he trailed kisses down the column of my neck.

"We have got to renegotiate your terms of employment," he murmured stopping to suck on a sensitive spot on my neck that immediately triggered my canines to elongate.

"Yes," I cried out wanting so much more than I knew how to ask for. I shook my head a little trying to bring some clarity. "Wait, I thought you were fine today, completely unaffected."

"Luce, does this feel like I've been unaffected?"

I gasped when he guided my hand to his steel hard length. I had never felt a man in the palm of my hand before and I realized I wanted more. I wanted to feel him. I needed to make him as crazy as he was making me. I wanted everything with Micah.

With my free hand I pulled his face back to mine so I could kiss him, but my hand continued to explore him as he jolted, and it felt like he grew impossibly bigger.

His breaths were starting to become more ragged. I was doing that to him, and it left me with a heady feeling.

"If you keep that up, I'm going to have to run home for a change of pants before my next appointment."

"Then take them off already," I said.

My cheeks grew instantly hot as I realized I'd just said that aloud.

He stared at me for a moment, almost as shocked as I felt.

"Are you sure?" he asked me.

I didn't hesitate as I bit my lip and nodded.

He stared at my mouth like he was in a trance as he removed his pants and then his underwear too standing before me in nothing but a shirt.

"Now you're entirely too overdressed," he said in a husky voice as he reached for me.

Micah had already been my first kiss and I wanted him to be my first everything.

"I'm not claiming you here in the office, but I need you so badly. Say yes, Lucy."

His hand skimmed down my arm stopping to toy with the hem of my shirt.

I nodded. "Yes."

Micah's smile lit up the room as he stepped closer to kiss me some more. His hand slid beneath my shirt and then up, gliding across the smooth skin of my abdomen. It tickled just enough to make me squirm in his arms.

As he cupped my breast and ever so lightly brushed his thumb against my nipple, I thought I would explode. I would soon learn that was only the beginning of it.

He carefully removed my clothes. I felt more exposed than ever, but it didn't scare me, no, it was thrilling.

His mouth and hands seemed to be everywhere. His hand slid down between my legs to toy with me. It was a strange sensation and I found it hard to stay still. But when first one finger, and then another invaded me, I gasped.

He smiled down at me. "Relax Lucy. I'm going to make you feel so good."

His hand was moving in and out of me making my head spin in new sensations.

"Yes!" I yelled.

"Please!" I begged, not even knowing what I was begging for.

My body was strung so tight.

I reached out for him wanting to make him feel just as good as he was making me. On instinct I started to stroke him. His groan only encouraged me to explore further.

I felt greedy with need, but I wanted to bring him along for the ride with me.

"Shit!" he exclaimed as one hand reached for mine tearing it away from him and pinning it to the wall above my head.

Before I could protest, his mouth found my breast and his fingers hit a spot inside me that had me screaming in sheer bliss. My body started to convulse, and my toes curled. Then just as quickly, I felt as if I were floating in darkness surrounded by only the scent of him.

I opened my eyes to find him staring down at me in wonder. He grinned and gave me a gentle kiss.

"Why'd you stop me?" I asked him.

"Oh, sweetheart, we're just getting started."

I squealed as he lifted me off the ground and I wrapped my legs around him.

I grinned and kissed him when it brought him right to my core.

I shivered unsure I could take anymore.

"Are you okay?" he asked staring at me with concern.

"Never better. I've just, uh never done this before."

At first he looked a little confused by my omission, I mean I did have a kid, but he also knew I hadn't conceived her naturally.

"Shit!" he finally said as he put it altogether.

He started looking around the room and I could feel him pulling back.

I grabbed his face and pulled it back to me. "Don't you dare stop now. I want it all and I want it with you."

He nodded. "But not here."

He held me tighter with one arm and reached for the door with the other. We streaked across the hall to one of the patient rooms where he laid me gently down on the table.

I giggled. "Here?"

"It's the closest thing to a bed I have. I'm sorry. If I had thought about it and realized…"

"There is no way you can possibly work like this," I said reached down between us and touching him.

"There are other ways to take care of that."

"Show me later," I said watching his eyes blaze.

He groaned and I thought he was going to stop, but then he nudged my thighs apart a little further and then he was there.

The second we merged as one, everything in my world felt right. This was where I was meant to be, maybe not quite there in the office on one of the patient tables, but with this man.

My heart swelled as he took me gently, ensuring everything was perfect for me.

This time when my body began to wire tightly, I had some inkling of expectation and it excited me. Still, I held off wanting to bring him with me. And boy was I glad I waited.

Watching Micah lose control and let go was the greatest thing ever and it brought me to new heights I never even dreamed of.

Neither of us wanted to open the clinic again after that. Micah was ready to call out for the day, but I knew we couldn't do that. This was his job and now mine too.

The rest of the day wasn't nearly so tense. We shared glances that made me blush, stole kisses between patients, and by the time I went to pick up Vada, I realized that I had never been happier.

It terrified me.

*****

Friday was much the same as we started finding our groove, and not just in the patient room across from his office that Micah had now blocked off for only absolute emergencies insisting on using just the other two rooms.

Turned out we worked really well together.

Everything was falling into sync for this picture perfect life. I could see it so clearly, but I wasn't perfect. I still had secrets and I wasn't sure how he was going to react if he ever found out.

There were people here who knew about me though, and they had accepted me. Maybe, just maybe he could too.

I wasn't sure I could risk my heart to find out though.

*****

At three o'clock I went to pick up Vada when Micah called.

"Missed me already? I've been gone all of five minutes. I'm not even to the school yet."

He chuckled. I loved that sound. It filled me with warmth.

"My last appointment just called and cancelled. I'm going to close up an hour early, so if you want, you and Vada can head on home. I'll bring pizza home for dinner so you don't need to worry about it."

"What? You're not sick of me yet?"

"That's never going to happen, Luce. But, you forgot, didn't you?"

"Forgot what?"

"Susan's picking you up at seven. You have ladies' night tonight and Vada and I have a date with pizza and a movie."

I pouted. Pizza and a movie sounded perfect.

As I pulled up to the school, I told him, "I'll just call her and cancel."

I didn't want to spend my Friday night with a bunch of women I didn't know.

"That is not happening. Besides, I was looking forward to having Vada all to myself."

How the hell was I supposed to say no to that?

*****

Ladies' night was unlike anything I could have imagined. There were more than a dozen women scattered around Kelsey's kitchen and living room. I did know several of the ladies there. Most, maybe even all of the Force mates were there, and I knew Kelsey, so that helped a little. I was quickly introduced to each one of them, though I could only remember the names of about half of them.

Around the room were probably eight or nine different conversations yet everyone seemed to be keeping up with all of them at once. My neck felt like I was witnessing a ping pong tournament as I looked back and forth just trying to keep up and they were all drinking wine and talking louder by the second.

"So Lucy, I hear you and Micah are mating?" Kelsey's sister, Elise, asked.

The entire room went instantly quiet, and all eyes were on me.

"You're Kelsey's sister, right?" I asked redirecting the question.

She shrugged. "Kyle's my brother, but close enough. I'll claim her as a sister any day. So are you?"

"Am I what?"

She glared at me. "Deflecting, I see. Are you mating Micah?"

"Uh, yeah, I guess."

"You guess?" Shelby asked. "You either are or you're not."

"They are," Susan confirmed. "Micah made that *very* clear at D&D this week."

The girl who worked on the Westin Force team, Taylor, laughed. "Tarron finally got you to go?"

Susan sighed. "Yes, and it was a lot of fun too, especially with Lucy there."

"You play?" Taylor asked.

I shrugged. "Someone taught a bunch of us when I was with the…"

My voice trailed off as Taylor's jaw set in a hardline.

"I remember," she said softly.

I knew she did too because she had been there at the end when they had come to rescue us all, or at least we had thought it was all at the time. I shivered, grateful for them all and happy to know the Raglan was completely dissolved and the human beasts behind it were dead.

"So you played while in captivity?" Elise blurted out.

I smiled. "Yes. It was like this whole other world we could escape too even if just for a moment. We didn't have the fancy dice or maps or anything, but we had our imaginations and sometimes it was just sitting in cages sharing a common story to pass the time and keep each other from going insane."

Shelby wiped her eyes and stood up to hug me. "That could have been my children's life too."

Her sister, Elizabeth, went to her side and wrapped an arm around her as she sobbed.

"I'm so sorry. I just hear all these awful things and I can't help but think how my babies were born into that world. It terrifies me."

"But they weren't. They were born into their daddy's arms and brought home to you," Elizabeth told her as the two embraced.

"I never let myself truly get upset or even sad about what had happened, and all I went through. Without it I wouldn't have my daughter and so I could never be fully angry about any of it. I got the best part of it all. Your kids never lived a second of that life. From what I heard, Ben delivered the babies and immediately took them away and brought them home to you."

I didn't dare say anything more. I couldn't talk about the helpless feelings of having your child ripped from your arms to disappear for hours of testing. They had been kinder to Vada than the others. I had done everything asked of me without complaint to ensure that.

They were all watching me. Staring. I didn't know what to say or do.

"So how about you and the sexy hot doctor? I hear you're working there now," Elise said making everyone laugh. The tension in the room instantly lifted as my cheeks turned a shade of dark red.

I didn't think I wanted to talk about Micah or our mating, until I opened my mouth to say so and things just started spewing out. I told them about how he had considered leaving the pack believing I must be mated. I explained how I hadn't wanted anyone to know about Vada's origins, but especially not him. I could say that in this group because I knew from the way Shelby had opened up that they were already aware and accepting of her children, which gave me hope that maybe they could accept my little girl too.

I talked about it. I told them everything, except the one secret I was still harboring even from Micah. And then even that was out there in the open.

"Does he know you're a healer?" Taylor asked.

My jaw dropped. My muscles tensed as I looked around the room. Much to my shock no one seemed surprised by the news.

"You all know?"

"I didn't know," Elise said. "Why didn't I know this?"

"Sorry. I really didn't think it was a secret. We celebrate witches around here, I guess I assumed that's how Kelsey convinced you to stay here," Taylor said.

"That's so sweet. You're a healer and he's a doctor. Just imagine what the two of you can do working together," Maddie said. She was one of Kelsey's brother's mates, or something like that. They were all a blur at this point.

"He can't find out what I am," I blurted out.

Kelsey came and sat next to me. It was almost surreal. I mean, I knew she was the Pack Mother, but the way the others scrambled to clear a path for her really highlighted the authority she had.

"Lucy, why haven't you told him?"

I shook my head. "I can't. I don't want to see that kind of disappointment or fear when he looks at me."

"You won't," Kelsey tried to tell me.

"You don't know that for sure. I've seen it too many times, even on people I thought cared about me. I can't risk seeing it from him."

"How does he not already know?" Shelby asked. "I mean, didn't he help out with the last mission?"

"No," Kelsey said. "He was supposed to go but was called to stay back at the last minute. I mean he did help, but from here, not onsite."

"I hadn't crossed paths with him until I took Vada to get her required school physical. Of that I am certain."

"If he's your true mate, then you would have known for sure," Elise said.

"There's no mistaking that call," Emma agreed.

"But it sounded like you weren't certain, so compatible mates? That's cool too, but you could have crossed paths with him at some point and maybe not have realized then. I mean there were a lot of shifters in one place, right?"

A small growl escaped me, and my eyes widened as I clamped my hand over my mouth.

"Nope, not compatible. Definitely true mates," Elise said with a smirk.

Micah

Chapter 12

I had always loved kids, but I had never really seen myself as a dad, until now. Vada was an easy kid to love. We spent a quiet evening of pizza and a movie, just like I'd told Lucy we would. After the movie, I got Vada cleaned up and into her pjs then we went back out into the living room so she could play a little longer.

I turned on one of the kid channels and laid down on the couch.

It wasn't long before Vada joined me.

"I seepy, Doc."

"Me too, sweetheart. Want to snuggle a bit before bed?"

She stared at me with her big eyes and nodded as she climbed up and settled onto my chest.

Before long we were both fast asleep and that's how Lucy found us.

Her gasp of surprise jolted me awake. She was staring down at us with an odd look on her face.

"Hey, you're home. Sorry, I guess I fell asleep." I gave her a sheepish look knowing Vada should have been in bed long before now.

Lucy still didn't say anything.

"Did you have a good time?"

She shrugged. "It was okay. Everyone was really nice."

I frowned. "Just okay?"

"It was great hanging out and relaxing. They sure do like their wine."

My wolf perked up unhappily. "You've been drinking?"

"Me? No. I just don't like it. Never have." She paused and looked at me weirdly again. "Would it have been a problem if I had?"

"If you had been drinking? No. Of course not. I just don't like the idea of you drinking and then driving. I know we're shifters, we actually burn off the alcohol faster than humans and a few beers isn't really going to impair anything, but during my residency I spent time doing rounds in an ER." I shuddered remembering the horrible needless suffering I'd witnessed in the name of just a few drinks. "I've just seen too much. It's not worth getting behind the wheel with even a drop of that stuff in your system."

She glared at me and then smiled. "I agree. And it's important to me to live that example for her." She pointed to the sleeping child on my chest.

"I completely agree."

I leaned down and kissed the top of Vada's head. I hadn't really considered such decisions for parenthood. I mean, I encouraged my patients, especially new parents, to think of these kind of things, but they had never directly affected me in the way they were now.

The realities of parenthood were hitting me hard, but how could I not think about it when all I wanted was a life with these two ladies.

Lucy was staring at us again with that look on her face that I couldn't understand.

"I know I should have put her down already. I'm sorry. She's just so cuddly."

Lucy smiled. "No, it's fine. A little extra love never hurt anyone."

She looked around the room and I wondered if she expected I would crash and burn flying solo with Vada.

"We survived alright," I told her as I sat up keeping the child close to my chest.

"I can see that. Everything's so tidy."

I shrugged. "Habit. In my line of work, it helps to keep everything in order."

She bit her lip, but I knew my obsessive tendencies had not gone unnoticed around the office either.

"I let her have fun and make a mess," I defended. "Then we played the clean-up game before getting jammies on."

She snorted. "Jammies? Clean-up game?"

I shrugged completely unaffected. Dealing with my youngest patients had always come naturally to me. Or maybe I'd just never fully grown up. My father would definitely agree to that one. My work ethics he never had an issue with. Turning over his practice had gone flawlessly. It was my personal life he'd always taken exception to.

"A grown man shouldn't play fantasy games all the time," he'd said on more than one occasion.

My mother didn't seem to care as much. She encouraged it even, but it drove my dad nuts.

Mom was more of a "When will you give me a grandpup? You know your father and I aren't getting any younger."

I looked down at Vada and grinned. Mom was going to love her.

"Hey, what are you two doing on Sunday?"

"Nothing that I know of, why?"

I stood up to take Vada to her room stopping to steal a kiss along the way.

"I'd like to take you and Vada to my parents' house for dinner, or really more like a really late lunch? Super early dinner? I don't know what to call it exactly."

While she thought about it, I disappeared down the hall and carefully laid Vada on her bed then tucked her in and kissed her sweet head.

"Sweet dreams, sweetheart."

Experiencing something so personal as putting a child to bed, not just any child, but my mate's daughter, did something to me inside.

I stood there a moment just staring down at her sleeping form.

Mine, my wolf whispered.

I grinned and nodded in the dark.

When I walked back into the living room, Lucy was pacing.

My heart started to pound as I looked around for any threats. Pacing was never a good sign for a shifter. It meant stress and anxiety.

"Luce, what's wrong?" I asked, going to her and wrapping her up in my arms.

"Your parents? You want me to meet your parents?"

I laughed. "Is that all? They're going to love you… both of you."

"Micah, I don't know if that's a good idea."

My heart dropped as I let go and stepped back to see her face.

"You don't want me as a mate?"

"That's not what I said."

"This is my family, Lucy. What am I supposed to think?"

"I don't do well with strangers."

"They aren't strangers, they're my mom and dad."

She sighed in frustration. "You don't understand."

"Then help me."

"My own mother took one look at my daughter and said get this abomination out of my house. We were left on our own out on the street. At that point in my life, I felt I was better off back in captivity with the Raglan than my own family. So forgive me if I'm not ready to just trust yours. She was my mother. She was supposed to protect me. Vada's her grandchild and she turned her back on us. They all did. The whole freaking pack, Micah. The Alpha apologized to us, but what the hell good was that?"

"Lucy, I am so sorry that happened to you, but my parents aren't like that."

"You can't know that for sure."

I shook my head. I couldn't fathom any circumstance that my parents would turn their back on me like that. Not ever. And not on me, my mate, or my child and my wolf and I had already claimed Vada as ours. I couldn't explain that to her though.

I gritted my teeth hating that she had gone through that. She had faced it all alone with an innocent baby. It wasn't right. I was here now, and I wasn't going away. They were mine to protect or die trying.

"You are mine, Lucy. Vada, is mine. I'm ready to claim you both and dare anyone to ever say such malicious things to you again. I'll rip their throat out."

Her eyes widened.

"Did you hear me? I want to claim you, Lucy. I want to spend the rest of my life with you and with Vada. I want us to be a family."

She shook her head and it felt like a knife was slicing through my heart.

"You don't mean that. You can't mean that."

"Do I look like I would joke about something like this?"

"I know you think you're doing the right thing, but you don't even know me, not really."

That hurt as much as her denying my claim.

"Don't know you? Okay. I get we haven't known each other that long, Lucy, but I do know you. I know you're an amazing mother. I know that despite you finding it humorous, you put up with my obsessive tendencies. I know every noise and whimper you make when I touch you. I know when you're watching me even when you think I don't. I know you were hurt, but I'm here to help you heal."

I took a chance and stepped closer to her. I needed to feel her in my arms, but she retracted and took a step back.

"This is going too fast. I need some time. I need space to think. I can't do that with you around. The bond makes me crazy with feeling things that cloud my judgement. I need to be away from you for a bit to think this all through and decide what's best for me and for my daughter, because no matter what I want, her needs take priority."

"That's what makes you such a wonderful mother," I whispered, even while feeling as though my heart was breaking.

"I don't think we should see each other this weekend. I'll see you at the office on Monday or I'll let you know my decision before then."

"I don't know if I can stay away," I confessed.

"Try," she said coldly.

I needed to punch something. I needed to yell and scream, but I couldn't take out my frustration on her. Not now when I knew she was scared and vulnerable. I was shaking inside, furious, hurt, and a little terrified I was going to lose her for moving too quickly.

Without another word and with tears starting to burn my eyes, I nodded and turned and walked out the back door, leaving my car there in her driveway. I shifted not even caring about destroying my clothes and then I ran.

My wolf stopped at the edge of the woods and turned back to the house one last time. Just like that first day when Vada had run outside, I saw Lucy's shadow in the window watching me.

My wolf sat and raised his nose towards the sky letting out the most soul crushing howl I'd ever experienced. He wanted his mate as much as I wanted mine. We'd never even seen her wolf, but I knew he could feel her presence because I could too.

I tried to force him to leave but my heart wasn't in it. Instead, he took control and peed a perimeter around her property warning off every other wolf in the Pack and marking her as ours because in human form, I hadn't been able to do the same.

It started to rain which seemed fitting for the melancholy feelings I was experiencing. Still, we stood there watching, knowing she was watching us back.

When the house went dark at last, my wolf finally turned and ran all the way home.

The second I was back in my skin, I wanted to call her. I needed to hear her voice and have her tell me everything was going to be okay.

I knew she was scared, but so was I, more now than ever.

I'd royally screwed things up just when I couldn't imagine life any more perfect.

*****

The next morning, I awoke after a restless night feeling like I was hungover, only I hadn't drank a thing. My head was pounding as I stumbled to the bathroom to find some Tylenol. I couldn't remember the last time I'd taken the stuff for myself, but I kept it here for emergencies.

"You just never know when you may need it, son," my father would say, so I had the stuff at the house, my car, the clinic, most anywhere there was a bottle on standby. This morning I was grateful for it.

I spent the bulk of the day sulking. I knew it too, but I wasn't going to stop it. Wallowing in self-pity seemed like a good idea for the moment. She had asked for the weekend. I had to give it to her, but I felt completely lost and hopeless without her.

It rained all day long only contributing to my foul mood.

I almost wished there was another baby ready to enter this world. I'd even take another breech one without complaint right about now. Anything to keep my mind off Lucy.

As night fell, I forced myself to go to bed for another restless night's sleep.

Sunday appeared to be much of the same, though the rain had stopped, and the sun rose high in the sky. I think I preferred the rain.

I was pacing a bare path in my carpet until at last my phone rang in the late afternoon.

"Lucy?" I asked without even looking at the caller information.

"No, it's Kyle."

My heart sank.

"Oh. What's up?"

"There's been a rockslide out by the old prison caves. Some teens were exploring up there. You know how intrigued they are by that place. We have two still missing and several injuries."

I sighed. I knew the place well. Even I had spent time exploring the caves our ancestors had used to constrain troubled wolves or punish them. The place gave me the creeps yet that's what kept people coming back to it. Some tried to say it was haunted. I knew it was mostly just a sad place.

I scoffed at the irony. A sad place for a sad pathetic wolf like me.

I grabbed my emergency bag and then realized my car was still at Lucy's. If the mud was bad enough to cause a rockslide, I knew it was better to use my truck anyway. I didn't drive it often, but it was there for emergencies just like this.

I drove over as close to the caves as I could get knowing I'd have to hike in the rest of the way. There were already a dozen or more trucks lined up. At a time like this, the Pack rallied together.

I jumped out, grabbing my med bag, and jogged the rest of the way. My boots were caked in mud and up ahead I could see Kelsey working on someone. I quickly ran to her side.

"What do we have?"

"Just a broken leg. I almost have it healed."

She gave me a weak smile and I looked around for Kyle, but he was working with a group to pull boulders away. I could see a foot sticking out through the mud.

"Shit. He didn't tell me it was this bad."

"Another collapse just after he spoke with you. There's three men still buried over there. I'm trying to get to them as quickly as I can. Where's Lucy?"

I paused for a moment not sure how to answer that. "At home with Vada."

It sounded like something normal to say. I didn't need Kelsey worrying about my state of mind or knowing how strenuous things were between us at the moment.

"When did you last eat?" I asked her.

"I don't know. Breakfast I guess."

I pulled out a protein bar and gave it to her.

"You'll be no good to any of us if you wear yourself out."

Kelsey was what we call a witch. Not like something you'd see on TV or even someone who practices witchcraft. A witch in the shifter world simply meant someone with extra powers. No one could explain why or how certain people obtained them. I assumed they were just born that way.

My Pack Mother had multiple gifts which were unheard of. I'd heard the stories of how she was born a triplet and inherited her sisters' powers after their deaths. She was fiercely powerful. I would never wish to showdown with her.

One of her many talents was healing. Healers should be celebrated as far as I was concerned. At times like this she certainly made my life a whole lot easier. I could set a broken bone and with our expedited healing powers it would be good as new in a few days as long as I did my job right, but Kelsey could mend it in a matter of hours, sometimes even less.

It took a lot out of her physically though. While I was more than happy to accept her help, it was also my job to ensure she didn't overdo it. Too much exertion of her powers always weakened her, sometimes for moments, sometimes for days. We had to maintain a balance.

The most critical cases I sent to Kelsey to stabilize. The things that weren't life threatening came to me. We made a good team.

"You're okay?"

"Fine. Go see Kyle. He'll fill you in."

"Don't overdo it," I warned her.

I ran over to discuss the situation with Kyle.

"Hey man. I just called Bravo team in to help, but I forgot they were leaving on a mission this morning and are already in the air. Delta team is about two hours out, but I'm not sure we can wait that long."

He went on to explain how they had found one of the boys but as they were pulling him out, another rockslide came down trapping the boy again and several others as well.

There are two almost out here, and at least four plus the kid up where the others are working.

I could see them steadily moving boulders and tossing them to the side.

"All rocks are being thrown to the right."

"Okay. Kelsey is stabilizing the last out here, so where can I help?"

Before Kyle could answer, someone in the upper section yelled down. "We need Doc. Got one, but he's not breathing."

I took off running before Kyle could give the order. I slipped a few times on my way up and I was covered head to toe in mud, but I got to work the second I saw my patient.

I never stopped to let it register who I was working on in a traumatic situation like this. It should never matter. My biggest priority was the patient in front of me. There weren't enough victims to warrant a triage approach, so one at a time.

I took a deep breath, assessing the situation. His airways were blocked. I opened his mouth and saw it was packed with mud. I was horrified by the site but I couldn't let myself react to it. Calm and steady. I cleared his mouth and checked his vitals. They were weak, but there. I immediately began chest compressions. He sputtered and choked as I rolled him to the side filled with relief.

This one had been easy. I only prayed the other cases would be as well.

"Are you okay?" I asked.

He nodded pointing back to the rocks. "Danny. My son."

I nodded. "He's still trapped in there?"

"Y-yes," he managed. "Help."

I motioned over for two men to assist him to safer ground, and then I went into the location he had pointed. "Hello?" I yelled.

"Help! Can you hear me?"

"Is that you, Danny?"

"Yes. I'm here. Help!"

I started digging in the mud passing large rocks I encountered. My hand finally broke through to the other side and the boy grabbed it.

"Help," he cried holding on to my hand for dear life.

I called onto my wolf and my free hand was suddenly covered in fur. The claws helped me move the wet dirt much faster. Steadily I worked until the boy was free.

A loud cheer went up.

"My friend. He's still in there. His leg was crushed by one of the boulders in the rockslide. I couldn't get it off of him. There was blood everywhere. I don't know if he's alive."

"Take him down. I'm going in for the other one."

"Doc, be careful."

"I will."

I forced my way through the hole which Danny had just come through. On the other side was a small pocket. I could even see one of the entrances to the cave. I wished I had thought to ask the friend's name.

"Hello?" I called.

I didn't get a reply but I heard a very slight grunt and moved towards it. I called up on my wolf once more to help my vision improve in the dark. I knew that was safer than using a flashlight at least until I found the kid.

That turned out to be easier than I expected. He was only a few feet from where the other had been but was pinned under a large boulder. It wasn't his leg, though. It was his arm, and I wouldn't be surprised if the bone was shattered.

I prayed that wasn't the case. The poor kid probably hadn't even gotten his wolf in yet. I'd hate to see him crippled and unable to ever shift. I shuddered at the thought. That was a fate worse than death for a shifter. I could only hope that Kelsey hadn't worn herself out too badly and had enough of her mojo left to heal him.

I moved the boulder away and he cried out in pain.

"That's a good sign, buddy. What's your name?"

Instead, I got something garbled and incoherent but it was a start.

I did a fast assessment to ensure there wasn't any other injuries that needed to be addressed before moving him. Then I pulled him up to his feet wrapping his good arm around my shoulder as I dragged him to our exit point.

Hands were waiting to assist on the other side.

"Careful," I yelled. "I need Kelsey to look at that arm quickly. It's bad, and he may have a concussion, but otherwise no visible damage."

I stayed behind him as I pushed him through until the others could grab him.

"Avalanche!" someone yelled.

I pushed with all my strength hoping to God that the kid made it through to the other side safe and sound because as rocks began to fall around me, I already knew it was too late for me. I cried out in pain as the structure above me collapsed and I drowned beneath the weight of the world shrouded in darkness.

Lucy
Chapter 13

I couldn't believe Micah had listened. My wolf was going insane. I was losing my mind. Vada was grumpy and irritable asking where Doc was every five seconds. I knew this was all my fault. I'd told him to stay away, but I never dreamed he'd actually listen. I had just been scared and freaked out when he wanted me to meet his parents. I knew it was stupid, but I couldn't help it. Experience had caused this, hard life lessons.

Where the hell was he?

I wanted to pick up the phone and call him, but my pride just wouldn't allow it.

He'd left his car here, surely he'd be back to get it.

I had barely survived through Saturday and by Sunday I could feel depression sinking in. I was ready to admit how very wrong I had been. Life without Micah was a million times worse than anything I'd ever lived through, and I was a survivor.

If I could overcome my past, then I could face anything, except a world without Micah.

I was ready to crawl to him on my hands and knees and grovel at his feet for forgiveness. I didn't just need him, I missed him as if half of me was simply gone. The worst part of all was that I wasn't sure he'd come back. I'd been pretty awful to him and no matter my reasons, it was time to face the facts.

Micah was my one true mate.

I was insanely in love with him.

By Sunday afternoon, I couldn't take it any longer. I packed Vada up and drove over to his house. I had only been there once to play Dungeons and Dragons, but I had a good memory and a keen mind for details, especially when they involved him.

I left Vada in the car and ran up to the porch to knock on the door.

Nothing.

I peeked in the windows. I called out his name. And I knew it was all a moot point because I couldn't feel his presence here and that scared the shit out of me.

Where was he?

I picked up the phone and called Kelsey. It rang four times, and I was about to hang up when she answered.

"Lucy?"

"Yeah, um, I'm really sorry to bother you, but I don't know who else to call. Micah and I had a really big fight after ladies' night, and I haven't heard from him since. I can't find him, Kelsey. It's freaking me out. I just need to talk to him."

"I thought you were going home to seal your bond?"

"He wanted me to meet his parents and I freaked out. I said some awful things and made him leave. What am I going to do?"

"You're going to set your pride aside and get your ass over here. There's been an accident, several rockslides at this point. Micah's onsite helping. I can't do this alone, Lucy. I need your help. I'm exhausted after this last healing and there are still more to come."

"Micah's there?"

"Yes."

"I can't, Kelsey, he doesn't know."

"I don't give a shit. I need you right now. Don't make me command you, Lucy."

"I have Vada here."

"Emma just got to Shelby's to watch the triplets. She's great with kids, I promise Vada will be safe there. Drop her off and Shelby will bring you here. But, Lucy, hurry."

"I'm already en route."

I had jumped back in the car the second she had said Micah was with her and was already driving. A few more turns and I pulled into Shelby's driveway.

There was a loud commotion on Kelsey's end. Everyone was cheering.

"What's going on?"

"Micah found the last boy we've been looking for. I think everyone might finally be accounted for, but there are so many injuries that I still need your help."

"Okay," I said hesitantly.

Emma appeared to have been waiting for me as she ran outside and snatched Vada from her seat. My daughter started to cry.

"She's fine," Emma said as Shelby slid into my passenger seat. "Go!"

"Do you need me to drive?" Shelby asked.

"No, I'm fine. Just tell me where."

As I was backing out of her driveway, it sounded like a bomb went off and I wasn't sure I was just hearing it through the phone.

"Kels, what happened?" Shelby asked.

"Oh my God!"

My heart sank and I knew something terrible had just gone down.

"Kelsey?" she tried again.

"The cave collapsed. They got the kid, but it doesn't look like Micah made it out. I have to go."

She disconnected the phone call, and I thought my heart stopped.

I was shaking all over.

"Pull over. Let me drive," Shelby said. "Lucy? Can you hear me?"

I nodded swiping at tears as they streamed down my face.

"I pushed him away. I told him I needed space. I was too chicken to tell him the truth. What have I done?"

"Lucy, this isn't your fault."

"I should have been with him."

"You will be. Turn here. Just up there. Park next to the trucks. Anywhere is fine."

As soon as I did, she jumped out of the car and then waited for me to follow. We ran up the hill. People were covered in mud from head to toe. I couldn't tell who was who and it didn't matter. They were working together as one moving debris and digging through the mud.

Kyle stood nearby barking orders, and everyone obeyed. It was like watching a machine at work until at last, there he was. They were pulling Micah out, and despite the caked on dirt, I knew it was him. I could feel him.

"I can feel him," I yelled to Shelby. "He's alive!"

I pushed my way up the hill even as they were passing him down. Arms reached out to stop me, but I pressed on. When I reached a safe landing, I demanded they set him down on the ground. It was enough to stall the well oiled pack machine.

Kyle looked down and saw it was me. He nodded and instructed them to listen to me.

They laid him down on the ground and I put out my hands to feel his life presence searching for any damage within his body.

A broken wrist was an easy heal.

A torn ACL took a couple seconds longer.

I moved up his body and cringed when I reached five broken ribs. I could feel my energy starting to wane, but I pulled what I needed from my wolf and together we mended them one by one.

Kelsey came over to see me.

"I have one left, a teen boy with a shattered arm. Lucy, he's never even shifted. We have to save him, but I'm worn down from the others. I need your help."

"But I have to save Micah. He should have woken up, but he's not."

"Is he stable?" she asked me.

I nodded hesitantly.

"Let me see." Kelsey held her hands out above him and then smiled. "He's going to be okay, Lucy, but this kid won't be without our immediate help."

I nodded. "Okay. It's what Micah would do."

"I'll stay with him, Lucy," Shelby said.

It took every ounce of strength I didn't feel I had to walk away from him.

"I need you fully focused, Lucy," Kelsey said.

"I know what we have to do."

I reached for her hand and held it tightly in mine. Together we merged our powers and concentrated fully on his arm. I could feel the shards begin to bind together. It took a lot of concentration as we couldn't afford to miss even one sliver or else this boy may never get a chance to shift. We couldn't let that happen.

Everything inside me screamed to go back to Micah, but I pushed it down and forced myself to focus. It took us over half an hour, but the worst was over. It was still broken and would take days, possibly weeks to fully heal, but we had managed to reconnect the pieces and set the shattered bone.

"He's going to be okay," Kelsey said as she sat back and wiped sweat from her brow. "I couldn't have done this without you."

"Lucy?" I heard Micah say.

I turned to find him leaning on Shelby as they walked slowly towards us.

"Missed his ankle," she said with a grin.

"Sit him down," I said turning back to the boy and checking him thoroughly one last time.

"He's good. We did it. Now go tend to your mate," Kelsey said.

I hesitantly walked back to Micah, but when he winced in pain as he knocked his foot trying to sit down, I ran to him and dropped down beside him.

"Where?" I asked.

"Inner ankle," Micah said through gritted teeth.

I cursed under my breath when I felt it. How the hell had I missed it?

I closed my eyes and let my powers resurface. I was exhausted from the healing, but this was Micah and I had to give it everything I had.

"You're a healer?"

I cringed not wanting to look up at him.

He jerked as a bone slid back into place.

"Sorry," I muttered.

"Hey, it's okay. I'm okay," he tried to say.

I still couldn't bring myself to look at him.

He reached out and touched my hand and I felt my powers flare bringing his ankle an instant healing like never before.

I turned to look at him. "Did you feel that?"

"Warm. It just felt warm."

"No, when you touched me, my powers spiked."

He nodded. "That's normal for true mates."

"Then why didn't Kyle help Kelsey?"

"Because she would have drained him of his Alpha powers and left the Pack vulnerable. They're a unique pair. She has to hold back careful not to pull too much of his powers through their bond even."

"You know about her? About healers?"

"Of course I do. Is that what you've been scared to tell me? Lucy, I'm not afraid of you being a witch. Are you kidding? Having a second healer around here would make my life a million times easier."

He gave me a sad look and I saw the hurt still evident in his eyes.

"Are you hurt anywhere else?" I asked him.

"Is that a trick question?"

The stab of guilt that shot through my heart was unexpected and completely justified.

Kyle walked over. "Hey, good work out there. Are you okay, man?"

"I'll be fine," Micah said. "How's Kelsey holding up?"

Kyle got a strange look on his face and his eyes sort of glazed over and then he burst out laughing.

"Um, let's see, mind your own business and heal quickly. She's fine."

He groaned. "Thanks for editing that for me. I'll check on her before I head home. Did we get everyone?"

"Yes, all's accounted for. I'm sending people home and this area is closed until further notice. I'll be issuing a full Alpha order on that today."

"Good idea. I'm glad everything worked out. Oh, wait, how's the kid I pulled out?"

"Doing well, thanks to Lucy. Kels says she couldn't have done it without you. Thank you."

My cheeks burned at the Alphas praise. "You're welcome," I managed to say.

I helped Micah to his feet, flourishing in the feel of his touch.

"You're really just okay with me being a witch?"

"Lucy, how many times do I have to tell you that there is absolutely nothing in this world that would make me not want you. I love you."

I stared at him in shock, as I stumbled.

A man reached out and steadied me. Much to my surprise, Micah didn't even growl at him.

"Easy there, young lady. Are you the healer who saved my son's life?"

"Maybe. Is he the one with the shattered arm?"

"No, he's the one you have yourself wrapped around."

"Dad, not now," Micah said shaking his head.

"What? I came as soon as I heard but looks like you two finished all the fun before I got here. Hi, I'm Mallick. Thank you for taking such good care of my boy."

"Um, okay."

I didn't know what to say. This was Micah's father.

"I've heard the rumors, of course, but I told your mother that there was no way they could be true, but my eyes are telling another story."

"Dad, this is Lucy," he said.

"I'm his mate and I'm a healer. Oh, and I have a daughter, Vada. She's two and she was conceived in a laboratory, and she is *not* an abomination."

I froze staring at him, unable to believe I'd just said all that to Micah's father of all people. I wanted to crawl under a rock and die.

The man looked from me then to Micah and back to me.

"Well, okay, then. Welcome to the family. His mother's been wanting grandpups for years. I do believe you just made her day. I suggest you both go get cleaned up and bring that sweet baby by to meet her grandparents already."

He turned and walked away.

"Did I really just say that?"

"Yes, you did, and seemed pretty proud of the fact too."

I groaned and covered my face to hide my embarrassment.

"Hey, Dad?"

"Yeah."

"Could we raincheck on stopping by? Maybe tomorrow?"

"No," Mallick said.

"Dad."

"What on Earth could be more important, son?"

"I need to go home, clean up, and then make this woman officially mine."

I gasped and looked up at him. He was grinning from ear to ear.

"Well, okay then. Breakfast tomorrow. Word travels quickly and I do not want your mother knowing I heard it first."

Micah chuckled. "Okay."

Shelby walked up next to me. "I'll just keep Vada for the night then. You can pick her up in the morning on your way to Mallick's house."

"Oh my gosh. You heard all that."

"Lucy, everyone heard you loud and clear."

I buried my face in Micah's shirt taking a second to breathe in his scent and let it ground me. I never wanted to be away from this man again.

"Are we really doing this?" I asked him.

He froze and I saw the fear in his eyes. "I'm not forcing this on you. You have a choice, Lucy."

"Then shut up and take me home."

"You're saying yes?"

"Absolutely. This weekend was awful, and I never want to fight again and…"

He silenced me with a kiss as those around us cheered, then he cradled me in his arms and carried me off into the sunset to mark me as his.

It was about time.

Micah

Chapter 14

I couldn't believe this was really happening. Lucy had basically just claimed me in front of the whole Pack, and she'd proudly proclaimed me, herself, and Vada to my father.

Of course, I knew her fears about my family were unfounded, but I also understood how deep the hurt and pain caused by her own family went. I made a personal vow to not let even a single day go by that she didn't know without a doubt that she and Vada were loved unconditionally by me.

I couldn't stop grinning as I drove her to my house. Aside from the time she'd showed up to play D&D, Lucy really hadn't spent any time at my home. I tended to go to hers where we had everything we needed for Vada.

I couldn't wait to bring my girls home, though it wasn't the time to discuss details such as that.

The house Lucy was currently staying in was a rental property on loan to her, thanks to Kyle. I owned mine outright and it was larger with more room for us to grow into as a family.

My heart was ready to burst with happiness at the thought of a forever future with my mate.

She looked a little confused and I could feel her nerves starting to rise as I pulled up in front of the house. I hated the uncertainty on her face.

"Luce, we don't have to do anything you aren't ready for. I will wait as long as I have to."

She turned to me and smiled.

"Just nervous. This is a big step."

I nodded. "I know."

She started to open the door and let herself out.

"Wait!"

I jumped out and ran around the front of the car to open the door for her. I offered her my hand. She grinned and shook her head as she took it.

Unable to stop myself, I pulled her into my arms and kissed her right there in the driveway.

She sighed and started to relax as she greedily kissed me back.

My lips didn't leave hers as I swooped her up into my arms and carried her into the house.

Pulling back, she looked around and sniffed the air.

"It smells like you, almost like the clinic but without the disinfectant odor."

I laughed.

"I hate that smell too, but it's necessary to keeping the place sterile."

"I know. I wasn't complaining."

I set her down, but her arms stayed wrapped around my neck as she pulled me back for another kiss.

My hands ran up and down her sides, but I could still feel a bit of apprehension within her, so I stepped back to give her a little space.

"Would you like something to drink? Sorry the place is a little messy. I'm not usually like this, it was just a really bad weekend."

She sighed and sat down on the couch.

"Some tea would be great if you have it."

"Sure. Be right back."

I walked into the kitchen to retrieve drinks from the fridge.

"There are two beer cans in here and a crumbled blanket and pillow on the couch. Is this really what you consider messy?" she teased.

I laughed.

"Yes," I admitted as handed her a drink and sat down beside her.

"You're too cute. Vada makes a mess ten times worse than this every five seconds, it feels like."

"I'm okay with that. It's the leaving it part that bothers me. I can get messy. There's a time and place for it. I mean look at me, I'm a mess right now, but drives me nuts to just ignore it."

She looked me over. There was dirt caked onto my clothes and under my nails. My hands were always spotless. I cringed as I noticed them now. Lucy saw it and a darkness crossed her face.

"Are you really okay? Today was a lot," she whispered.

"I know, and I really am. Thanks to you."

She shook her head.

"Lucy, you have a true gift. You can't deny it and you don't have to hide it, not here, and certainly not from me."

She sighed. "I should have told you sooner. I'm sorry. It's just always been this dark secret. Witches terrify people. Why isn't it bothering you?"

I relaxed and smiled. "I've had plenty of experience with witches. They fascinate me but I do make it a point of staying on their good sides."

I was just trying to make a joke but saw immediately that it fell flat.

"I would never hurt you."

"I know that. I'm not scared of you. I was only trying to make light of it, and I shouldn't have. I can't even imagine what you've had to deal with. It doesn't have to be a secret here, but if you prefer it that way then…"

She cut me off. "Then it's too late because half the Pack already saw me heal you and others today."

"That was hardly half the Pack."

Her jaw dropped in surprise. "How many people are in this Pack?"

"A lot. Even I don't really know, but it is the largest wolf shifter Pack in the world and if you add in all the other animals we have living here now, it's even bigger than that."

"I hadn't thought of that. Wow. That's insane."

I shrugged. "It's still a small town where everyone knows everything, so yeah, it would be hard to lock this down, but not impossible."

"It's fine. I mean, everyone knows about Kelsey here, right?"

"Definitely."

"So, I guess the wolf's out of the bag, and I'll just have to get used to it."

"I'm sorry we put you in that position. I'm sorry I put you in that position."

"You weren't the only one I worked on today. Kelsey was wearing out and needed me. She's done so much for me that I just couldn't tell her no."

"You did the right thing, and I'm not just saying that because you saved my life."

I gave her a lazy grin, but she just rolled her eyes before turning a wide-eyed serious look up at me.

"I've never been so scared, Micah. I thought I was going to lose you."

I rubbed her back gently and leaned in to whisper, "You aren't going to get rid of me that easily."

She reached up and caressed my cheeks reverently.

"I don't ever want to get rid of you. As terrifying as that is to me, it's true. I'm not used to relying on other people."

"Because they always disappoint or hurt you?" I guessed.

She nodded.

"I can't promise I will never disappoint you, Lucy. I can't even promise I'll never hurt you. I could never do either intentionally. But I am still human, at least partly, and I'm not perfect."

She shook her head.

"You are perfect, though. Perfect for me."

Overwhelmed by her words, I closed the gap between us and kissed her again. This time I deepened it, letting my tongue run across the seam of her lips until she smiled and opened to me. I nipped at her bottom lip before letting my tongue dance with hers.

When she let out a soft moan, I slowly pulled back. She looked a little dazed and confused as I stood up and then took her hands to pull her up to me. Before she could question my motives, I tossed her over my shoulder and walked down the hall to my bedroom.

As much as I wanted to just lay her down on the bed and claim her as mine, I detoured for the shower first. I turned on the water to let it warm and before she could stop me, I walked us both in, clothes and all, and finally set her down.

She shrieked and then laughed.

"Micah, you're crazy!"

"Come on, we're both disgusting and covered in mud. Tell me you didn't need this, too."

"You could have let me take my clothes off first."

She was fussing, but her face was bright with a smile and a twinkle in her eye.

"You're right. Let me help you with that."

Slowly, I started removing her clothes one item at a time. First her shirt, her shoes, one sock, then the other. I took my time undoing her pants and sliding them down her legs as I pressed a kiss to her stomach making her quiver. Her matching bra and panties I quickly peeled off to join the rest of her clothes on the floor.

I kicked off my shoes and socks and reached for the hem of my shirt, but she beat me to it as she slowly lifted it over my head. I laughed as she tried to tug the soaking wet shirt off of me. I moved to help, but she smacked my hand away determined to do it herself. She grinned triumphantly when she finally managed to get it over my head and tossed down on the floor of the shower. Then she let her hands trail down my body until she reached the button of my pants.

Starting to get impatient, I let her undo the button and unzip my pants before I took over and pushed them down along with my boxers and kicked them to the side.

My mouth found hers again and as my tongue ran across her teeth, I felt her canines begin to shift and smiled against her lips.

"Not yet, my sweet mate."

She pouted, making me laugh.

"I am not claiming you in the shower, but I do have other plans."

With an evil grin, I kissed her pouty lips.

Her arms wrapped around my neck as I lifted her and then backed her against the wall. When the cool tiles hit her back, she arched right into me, exactly where I wanted her.

In this new position I wasted no time easing her down on me as I took her hard against the shower wall.

Her moans spurred me on.

The scrape of her nails down my back made me heady in a powerful way.

Being with Lucy made me feel invincible. It was the one place in my life I knew without a doubt that I belonged. A few days away from her had made me see that clearly and I didn't want to go another day without her.

"You're mine," I told her with a growl as I started to feel myself coming unhinged.

"Yes!" she cried out.

I could feel her tightening around me and I kissed her as her body began to quiver. I couldn't hold out much longer. One thrust, two, and I was following her over that cliff into ecstasy.

Despite my shaking limbs, I continued to hold her as our heartbeats began to slow.

Neither of us said a word. We just stood there. My body pressed against hers as hot water rained down on us.

Two hearts beat as one as we stared into each other's eyes.

I may not have physically marked her, but I'd claimed her none-the-less. The dynamic shift drawing us closer was tangible. This was it.

Quickly, I grabbed a bar of soap and started lathering it across her body. Her little murmurs and mews told me she was still very much turned on and I could already feel myself growing hard again.

She took the soap from me and returned the favor. I loved the feel of her hands running across my body.

By the time we were clean I wasn't even sure I was going to make it to the bed before making her officially and forever mine.

Lucy

Chapter 15

Standing there drying off in his bathroom, I couldn't stop grinning. I should be nervous, but I wasn't. Almost losing him had reminded me just how short life could be. There were a lot of things I was still uncertain about, but Micah wasn't one of them.

After Vada was born, I'd made a promise to her and myself that I wouldn't make rash decisions, that I'd think through my choices thoroughly, and not act emotionally. I had to do what was right for her.

I stole a glance at my mate. If he wasn't what was best for the both of us, then I didn't know what was.

Micah was so much more than I'd ever dreamed possible. He was kind and nurturing. He loved openly and wasn't afraid to show affection. That wasn't only to me, but to my daughter as well.

When he looked at her, he didn't see an abomination. He didn't see a broken, irreparable kid. He just saw her. He lit up when he saw her and I had no doubt that he was going to be an amazing father and protect her as his own.

He walked over and wrapped his arms around me. As I watched us in the foggy mirror, he started kissing me down the column of my neck and across my shoulder, then back until at last he stopped and sucked hard on one spot.

My stomach twisted with excitement knowing that was where he was going to mark me to seal our bond forever.

Nerves? Nope. I was filled with excitement and hope.

My canines started to elongate in anticipation, and I smiled showing him through the mirror.

He gasped and then growled. It was the sexiest sound I'd ever heard.

My phone dinged.

Just ignore it, Lucy. This is too important of a moment.

I turned in his arms and pulled him down to kiss me. I could feel the sharp points of his canines too as I grinned against his lips.

This was it.

My heart raced as he lifted me up into his arms.

My phone dinged again.

I paused for only a second, brushing away the seed of worry settling into the pit of my stomach.

When it chimed a third time, Micah set me down on my feet halfway to the bed.

I looked up at him in confusion.

"Something could be wrong. You have to check it."

"But…" I started to protest even while running for my phone in relief.

It was back in the living room. If it wasn't for our stupid accelerated hearing, I wouldn't even have noticed it.

"Is everything okay?" Micah asked. I could feel his apprehension combining with mine as I opened my messages.

My shoulders slumped.

"No. Apparently the kids somehow snuck a big bag of candy and between the four of them they ate the whole bag. Vada puked twice already."

Micah didn't say a word as he walked back to the bedroom and returned only a few minutes later fully dressed in clean clothes and handing me a pair of sweatpants and a sweatshirt.

"Sorry, but you don't have any clothes here yet. It's the best I can offer."

I looked at him through eyes filled with love.

"Shelby says she's okay but just felt she had to say something. Should we finish this first?" I asked hesitantly, even knowing that for me, my concern over Vada trumped even something as important as mating this man.

"Luce, our baby is sick. She needs you. Get dressed. We can swing by the house if you want your own clothes, but we both know all we're going to do is worry about her. We have our entire lives ahead of us. This is going to happen, just not tonight."

"You're sure?"

"Put the clothes on and come on. Of course, I'm sure."

Feeling relieved, I slipped on the soft sweats he'd handed me, loving being covered in his scent.

He grabbed my hand, and we ran to the car like we were our way to an emergency.

"Did she say anything else? How many times has she thrown up?" he asked once we were sorted in his truck because his car was still back at my house.

"Twice. I'm sure she's fine, just an upset stomach from too many sweets," I tried to assure him as much as myself. "She's never really been sick before."

He reached over and squeezed my hand.

"Do you need to go home first?"

"No. I'd rather just get to her and see how she is for myself."

"Thank God. I was hoping you'd say that."

I grinned.

"Are you okay?" I asked him.

"I don't know. I mean I handle dozens of cases like this all the time. It's one of the most common ailments for shifter kids, but this is Vada. It just feels different. My wolf is on edge."

"Probably because he was expecting something different for this evening," I teased, finding it helped my own nerves a lot to share this with him.

I didn't feel so alone for once.

He shook his head adamantly.

"My wolf and I are in full sync and know she comes first. She has to. She's just an innocent child and it's not going to change anything to wait a few hours or a few days to complete our bond, but I'd never forgive myself if something happened to that little girl."

"I love you!" I blurted out.

He had said the words to me, but I'd never returned them. As those three powerful little words left my lips, I felt the truth of them all the way to my toes.

"I do," I continued. "And I love that you're putting my daughter first over your own needs, even over my needs, because I do need you, Micah. That's not easy for me to admit, but I do need you."

He pulled up to Shelby's drive and parked the car then turned to me. His hands captured my face as he stared into my eyes.

"I don't just want to mate you, Lucy. You two are a package deal. I know that. I want it all, our little family, and Vada's an important part of that. She's so small and innocent. I'm not saying I won't want time alone with you. Of course I do, but she's just a child and right now she needs you."

Tears filled my eyes as I nodded and smiled.

"I love you so much," I told him and then I kissed him.

He pulled back and smiled. "I love you too, now let's go and get our girl."

I couldn't stop smiling as we got out of the car and walked up to knock on the door. Shelby looked frazzled when she answered.

"No, no, no. What are you doing here? I told you we had it under control."

"Mary Alice just went down," her mate yelled from down the hallway.

"Oh no."

She turned and took off running, so we followed.

There was a pile of blankets on the floor with bowls lined up. One of her boys grabbed for one and threw up.

They all looked miserable.

"You're sure it was just candy?" Micah asked.

The man pointed to the pile or wrappers in the corner. "We're sure."

He chuckled. "Wow. That's an impressive pile. Lucy, have you met Ben yet? Ben, this is my mate, Lucy."

"Hi. I'd shake your hand, but trust me, you don't want me to do that."

"I'm so sorry."

"Don't be. Seriously. They asked, I said no. I should have made sure it was better out of reach."

"It was on the top shelf, babe. These little masterminds worked together and were determined. I'm pretty sure they will rule the world someday at this rate, especially adding Vada into the mix. That is one smart cookie you have there."

Even though I felt horrible about the situation, it was really nice to see my daughter interacting with other kids, kids that were just like her.

"Mommy?" Vada's little voice said as she lifted her head from the pillow.

"Hey sweet girl, mommy's here."

She got up and walked over to me, but then detoured at the last second to Micah. He didn't hesitate to scoop her up into the safety of his big strong arms.

"My tummy hurts, Doc."

"I know, sweetheart. We're going to get you home so you can rest and feel better." Then he turned back to Shelby and Ben. "BRAT diet. Bananas, rice, apples, and toast. Keep it simple for the next twenty-four hours. And keep them hydrated. This should pass quickly and that will be easy on their poor bellies. We're really sorry this happened."

"Kids will be kids. I'm just sorry we interrupted your night," Shelby said. "Did you?"

Lucy shook her head. "Not yet. But some things are more important."

I stroked Vada's back and kissed her little hand as she clung to Micah and then turned to reach for me.

She buried her face in my neck and sniffed.

"You smell like Doc," she announced making me blush.

"If you're willing to trust us not to allow this to happen again, she's welcome over here anytime," Ben told us. "Really. They had a blast right up until the second they started paying the consequences of a really bad decision."

We all laughed.

"Thank you both. Really." I said as I let Micah guide us out.

"Call if you need anything at all. Dehydration is really the biggest concern and when they're ready to eat again, just stick to the BRAT diet and they'll be fine."

"Thanks, Micah," Shelby said.

The sound of a dry heaving kid was in the background.

"Not again," Shelby cried as she ran back to her children.

As we reached the truck, Micah stopped and swore under his breath.

"What's wrong?"

"I don't have a car seat for her."

"It's fine. I'll just hold her."

He looked at me like I was insane.

"Micah, we have to get her home."

Reluctantly he agreed.

"Just hold her tight. Maybe strap the seatbelt around the both of you."

I laughed. "We've been through so much worse than a five-minute car ride without a car seat and survived. Just watch the road and drive. It'll be fine."

The five-minute car right took us fifteen minutes as he refused to go over fifteen miles an hour.

"I'm pretty sure we could have walked home faster," I teased.

He put the truck into park and glared at me.

"We're here safe and sound. That's the important part."

"You have a protective streak; did you know that?"

He rolled his eyes. "Only since the two of you walked into my clinic."

I blushed remembering that day.

"I didn't exactly handle that well, did I?"

He laughed. "No, you didn't."

Vada started to heave again interrupting our walk down memory lane.

Without hesitation, Micah took her from me and left the truck. Then they both disappeared. I jumped out to find him squatted down while balancing her on his knees. One hand supporting her chest while the other rubbing her back.

"It's okay, sweet girl. Just let it all out," he told her softly as she vomited again.

I cringed and took a step back. I really hated to deal with puke, but he didn't seem to mind it at all.

"Better?" he finally asked as she nodded weakly. Without even looking my way he spoke again. "Mommy, we got a little on her shirt, can you get a fresh outfit and maybe draw a warm bath? I don't know about you, Vada, but a warm bath always makes me feel better."

"Me too," she assured him.

I held my hand to my chest as I watched the two of them before forcing myself to go inside and get things ready. With fresh pajamas laid out and the tub filling with warm water, Micah walked in with Vada. He carefully undressed her and then settled her down into the tub.

She seemed to perk up a little as she splashed in the water, but she still looked a little miserable.

"How are you feeling sweet pea?" I asked.

"Hungry," she surprised me by saying.

"Well, that's a good thing," Micah said. "Mind if I dig around in the kitchen while you two finish up here?"

I cringed knowing I hadn't gone shopping and there was very little food in the house.

"Um, sure, but I probably need to make a run out."

He didn't say anything as he disappeared from the room.

I squatted down and washed her quickly.

"You ready to get out, Vada?"

"Yes, pease."

She held her arms up for me to pick her up and wrap her in a towel. I held her to me breathing in her sweet baby scent and assuring myself she was okay.

I grabbed her pajamas and walked to her room to change her there instead.

Before long something wonderful started smelling up the whole house.

"What is that?" I asked as I picked Vada up and carried her to the kitchen.

Micah was standing at my stove cooking something.

"Did you run out to the store?"

"Nah. You had all the basics we need to make our princess feel better."

"I did?" I asked skeptically.

"You did."

He motioned for us to sit as he dished a small portion of rice and some applesauce for Vada. She dove in without complaint, something that rarely happened.

Then he set a plate in front of me that made my mouth water. Rice, chicken, and applesauce. It was so simple but smelled amazing.

"Good, Doc," Vada praised. "Tummy all better."

"Not quite munchkin, but it's a start. Let's see if you can manage to keep that down."

I took a bite of the rice, closed my eyes and moaned in appreciation.

When I opened my eyes, Micah was staring at me with a heated look in his eyes.

"I have a feeling I'm going to be cooking a lot more often if that's the response I get."

I blushed but I wasn't going to complain if that was a job he wanted to take over.

"Why don't we call it a night?" I finally said. "This little lady could use a good night's sleep."

Micah seemed hesitant but nodded.

"I'll clean up while you put her down."

"No, Doc!" Vada surprised me by saying.

"Um, how do you feel about baby duty instead?"

"I not a baby," she insisted.

"No, you aren't," Micah told her as he took her from me and headed to her room.

I got up and cleaned up. He was great about cleaning as he went about his day. I'd noticed it at work and at home.

Once done, I sat down on the couch, exhausted from quite possibly the longest day of my entire life. After a few yawns I knew I needed to go check on things before I fell asleep right there.

In the nursery, I found Micah half snoozing with Vada fast asleep on his chest. Somewhere along the way he'd stripped off his shirt and was only wearing his sweatpants. I gulped at the sight as my heart lurched in my chest.

"Hey, she's asleep." I started to take her from him, but his eyes looked a little wild and uncertain. "She's okay," I assured him.

"But what if she wakes up sick in the night? Maybe I should just stay here and keep an eye on her."

I couldn't help but smile, feeling grateful at the love and care he showed her.

"You can stay if you want."

"I can? I mean we never discussed it, so I didn't want to assume."

"Micah, if we hadn't been interrupted, we'd already be fully mated by now. Unless you're having second thoughts, then I guess we need to start talking about it."

It made me nervous, but not scared anymore. He was mine and one thing I knew with certainty was that I fought for what was mine.

"Come on," I said, taking his hand.

I'd expected him to put Vada down in her bed, but instead he kept one hand in mine and the other carefully holding her.

"Are you keeping her with you all night?" I teased as I let go of his hand and crawled into bed.

"Can I?" he asked.

"Don't make a habit of this," I warned him as he settled into bed beside me carefully cradling her to his chest as he used his free arm to snuggle me into his side.

Everything about this moment affirmed to me that this was the man I was meant to share my life with. It terrified me just how much I trusted him, and I prayed he never broke the faith I was placing in him.

As the full reality of all that had happened today came crashing in around me, I didn't freak out like I normally would have. I didn't cry. I didn't let it draw me into the darkness of despair. Instead, I embraced it, took comfort in my mate, and drifted off into the best night's sleep I'd had in a very long time.

Micah

Chapter 16

Vada stirred against my chest with a big stretch.

I peeked one eye open to look down on her and then slowly opened the other. My hand rubbed her little back and when she didn't squirm in discomfort, I knew the candy eating incident was behind us.

Lucy was awake and watching me. I could feel it.

I turned my head until our eyes met, overwhelmed by the love I saw there.

"What time is it?" I asked, then leaned over and kissed the top of her head.

"Seven."

"Shit. We have to get moving."

"But the clinic doesn't open until nine."

"Yeah, but I promised Dad we'd stop by for breakfast first."

"Oh."

"I may go ahead and close today for emergencies only. Given everything that happened yesterday, no one will blame me."

She frowned. "That's not a very good business model."

I groaned. "Now you sound like my dad."

"Do we really have to go? Can't you call and explain that Vada was sick last night?"

I nodded. "I can do that, but it's only putting off the inevitable, Luce. I'm close with my family and they're going to love you, both of you."

"You can't know that for sure."

"I know you're scared, and trust me, if they do anything that makes you uncomfortable, I will grab you both and get the hell out of there. They are important to me, but not as important as the two of you."

"You're sure about this?"

"It's going to be fine. My mother is going to love you, both of you," I added, knowing that was her real fear.

She could deal with my parents not accepting her, but not accepting her daughter was unacceptable. I loved that about her. She was one fierce mama.

It took some convincing, but I did manage to get her moving. And soon we were pulling up to my childhood home with the big front porch overlooking Main Street. Across the street was the park and the pond where I'd spent a large portion of my time growing up.

With a bit of coaxing, Lucy reluctantly got out of the car. I didn't hesitate to usher her inside, not even stopping to announce our presence, though I had no doubt they were waiting for us.

Dad met us in the foyer.

"Is it done?"

I scowled in frustration.

"No, but it will be soon. Vada got sick."

"Sick? Shifter kids rarely ever get sick," he said, sounding concerned.

I smiled. "They do when they get into a big bag of candy and eat it all. Apparently, Vada and the Shay triplets are a bit of trouble together."

He laughed. "Poor kids. Is she okay now?" he asked, addressing Lucy instead of me this time.

"I think so. She only puked once since we picked her up and did manage to eat a little bit of dinner last night before bed."

"Good. Good. You're keeping her on a BRAT diet?"

"Yes, sir."

I laughed. "Dad, relax. I can handle this."

"I know, son. But I'm allowed to be worried about my only grandpup, aren't I?"

Lucy stiffened next to me.

Instinctively, I reached over and rubbed her back to calm her nerves.

"Can I hold her?" he finally asked, taking Lucy by surprise.

"Um." She looked up at me for direction.

I nodded.

"Okay," she said as she carefully handed her off.

"It's Vada, right?"

"I Vada," she told him proudly, stealing his heart in an instant.

"Hi Vada. I'm your grandad."

The child reacted to the title and looked hesitantly over to her mother.

"It's okay, sweetie. He's nice," she assured her, though I could still sense uncertainty wafting off her.

"Vada, this is my daddy," I explained.

"Oh. Doc's daddy?"

"Boy do I have someone who's going to be excited to meet you."

"Who?" she asked.

"Your grandma."

Vada pulled away from him and shook her head.

I reached out and took her from him, wanting to shield her from all of this.

"I'm sorry," Lucy said. "Grandma was what I referred to my mom as. Let's just say, things didn't go well."

I sensed her embarrassment at the admittance.

"That wasn't your fault."

"I know, but well…"

"You know what? How about we come up with better names instead then?" Dad suggested.

"Thank you," I mouthed.

"Vada, Micah's grandfather is called grandpappy. What do you think of grandpa for me instead of grandad?"

"Grandpa Doc?" she asked.

My father smiled triumphantly, completely smitten by her.

He held out his hands and she accepted the offer to return to him.

"Grandpa Doc it is."

"Mallick? Who's at the door?"

"Come on," I said, placing a hand on Lucy's lower back and ushering her forward.

"Mom," I said, as she looked up at the sound of my voice.

Tears started to fill her eyes as she stood there in the kitchen wearing her apron and baking, with a little flour on her left cheek.

"I've heard the rumors, you know? I just didn't want to get my hopes up."

I smiled proudly. "Mom, this is Lucy, my mate. My true mate," I clarified.

She came around the kitchen island and pulled Lucy from me as the two women embraced.

"I've been praying for you for so long. Let me look at you. Micah, she's gorgeous," she gushed, not telling me anything I didn't already know.

"Yes, she is."

Lucy was blushing furiously.

Mom sniffed her and then frowned.

"What's the hold up? Why haven't you sealed your bond already?"

I chuckled. "Trust me, I'm trying. Vada had other plans."

"Vada? What's Vada got to do with anything? Wait, she didn't go into labor this early, did she?" Mom asked.

"Oh, no. Sorry. I didn't mean to worry you. That Vada is just fine."

"Vada's my daughter," Lucy said.

Mom turned big watery eyes up to me and I nodded.

"You're bringing me home a daughter and a grandpup to love?"

"I am. She's in the living room wrapping Dad around her little finger."

Mom started to leave.

"Wait," Lucy said.

Mom stopped and looked back with concern.

Lucy squared her shoulders and jutted out her chin in defiance.

"Vada wasn't conceived like a normal child. I was held in captivity at one of the Raglan facilities when they impregnated me with her. She was created in a lab, and I don't know what that means for her future."

"Just like Shelby and Ben's kids?"

"Exactly like the triplets, Mom."

I was proud of Lucy for facing her fears head on even while I knew that wasn't necessary for my parents. Still, it was important for my mate.

I wrapped an arm around her encouraging her to continue.

"That scares a lot of people. We were rejected by my family and by my Pack, which is partly how we ended up here."

"And you fear we're going to reject her too?"

Lucy slowly nodded.

"Mom, they've been through a lot…" I started but she cut me off.

Taking Lucy's hand in both of hers, my mother looked at her fiercely.

"So much pain and hurt. It breaks my heart. I'm a firm believer that every child, regardless of how it was conceived, is a blessing from God. Vada is special and she is lucky to have such a strong mother to look after her."

She reached up and lifted her chin until their eyes met.

"I am sorry that your family and your Pack couldn't understand that. As a mother, I understand your fierce need to protect her and Mallick and I would be honored to stand by your side in that battle. Let anyone speak even an unkind word about my grandpup and they'll have me to answer to."

Lucy's shoulders shook as she started to cry. It wasn't a little cry, but a full body-wracking ugly cry. I stepped aside as my mother embraced her and then shooed me away.

I felt helpless leaving her so upset, but with one last stern look from my mother, I found myself backing out of the room.

"Everything okay?" Dad asked.

I ran a hand through my hair. "I think so?"

"That girl's been through a lot."

"Too much," I agreed. "I hate it, like I somehow let her down because I wasn't there to shield her from it."

"She's strong, son. All she needs is love and time."

I nodded in agreement.

"Mommy okay, Doc?"

"Yeah, sweetie, Mommy's going to be just fine. Are you having fun with Grandpa Doc?"

Her face lit up and she nodded.

"He gave me candy," she whispered.

I scowled at my dad.

He stopped me before I could scold him.

"Relax son, just a piece of peppermint. It's good for belly aches."

I sighed, unable to argue with that.

"You already knew all about Vada, didn't you? Before Lucy blurted it out yesterday?"

"Yup," he confessed. "I may have retired the title of Pack Physician over to you, but I am still on the Pack Council."

"So the whole Council knows?"

He nodded. "Kyle keeps us informed on all the new shifters moving into territory."

"Were there any concerns about my girls?"

"None. We all accepted Ben's request to adopt those babies of his, and Vada here is no different. She's just an innocent child, son."

"I know that, Dad. And I know that I will do everything in my power to protect her."

"She's your daughter now. Or she will be if you ever get around to sealing your bond with that mate of yours."

I groaned and rolled my eyes.

"I'm trying."

"You're always welcome to leave this cutie pie here with your Mom and me. We're happy to babysit anytime."

"Thanks."

I was still trying to absorb what he had said. I have a daughter now. Vada was my daughter. I looked down at her and grinned.

"You're mine, kiddo," I whispered.

"You mine, Doc," she said as she threw herself into my arms.

Dad nodded his approval as I hugged my baby girl.

I didn't know if she realized how much her words meant to me, but I like to think she truly meant them.

"Kids. They'll soften even the toughest sonofabitch."

I was fighting back emotions but couldn't help but laugh at his words. They certainly resonated as truth to me.

"You always were good with little ones. You're gonna make a hell of a great father."

I looked over at him with pride.

"I had a pretty great role model."

Lucy

Chapter 17

I don't think I have ever cried as much as I did in Micah's mother's arms. It was like the woman knew exactly what I needed to hear, like she was speaking straight to my heart.

I had no idea how long I stood there in her kitchen bawling and spilling everything I never dreamed of telling another soul, not even Micah. It was like she unleashed a flood door within me, and everything came pouring out.

When at last my tears had run their course, she squeezed me harder.

"There, there. All better now?"

Certain my eyes were puffy and my face blotchy, I wanted to hide back in the comfort of this woman's arms. But I straightened up and stood tall as I nodded.

"I'm so sorry."

"Do not ever apologize for your emotions. Do you hear me?"

I nodded.

"I can't imagine the relief of getting all of that off your chest. If anyone ever needed a good cry, it was you."

"I don't know what came over me." I was suddenly embarrassed.

"You aren't alone anymore, Lucy. And you don't have to carry this burden alone."

I nodded as tears threatened to flow once more.

"Would you like to meet my daughter?" I finally asked.

"I would love that."

Despite everything we'd talked about and all I'd shared with this woman, I was still nervously waiting on pins and needles for her to banish us from the house and call my child an abomination. I knew in my heart that Micah's mother was nothing like my own, but still, I couldn't bear it.

Had Mallick rejected us, that would have been hard, but to have one more woman, a mother, turn her back on us, would be more than I could handle.

I watched her as we walked into the room, and she saw Vada for the first time. Unshed tears filled her eyes.

"Hi sweet girl," she said, taking the seat that Micah quickly vacated to stand by my side.

"Are you okay?" he asked.

"I think so. I'm sorry I broke down like that. I'm not usually like this."

He pulled me into his arms and held me.

"I should have told you and explained things better. Instead, I just unleashed on your mother."

He chuckled. "She has that way about her. And you've told me enough for me to understand. Remember, I've been privy to so much more than the average person that it sadly doesn't shock me anymore. We have people here you can talk to, if you want. Mom's a great start though."

I turned to watch her interact with Vada.

"Who are you?" my daughter asked.

"I'm your grand…"

Mallick cut her off.

"This is my mate. Doc's mom."

"Doc's mom? Grandma Doc?"

I was surprised when she didn't flinch as she said the name. I'd played up the whole grandma thing on our journey home. I had honestly thought everything would be okay and we'd be safe again. How very wrong I'd been. Grandma was now associated with a big fat negative in our lives.

I looked up to Micah. He smiled and kissed my forehead.

"Dad and I were discussing it with her, trying to explain that not all grandmas are bad. We were leaning towards Nanny instead, but if she's okay with it, it might be good for her."

I hugged him tighter and closed my eyes saying a quick prayer of thanks for having him in our lives.

"Thank you," I whispered.

As I watched Lorraine play peek-a-boo with her until Vada was laughing so hard that Micah had to swoop in and rush her to the bathroom, I knew he had been right. They were different and not all people were going to see her in a bad way.

"Sorry. I guess we got a little carried away."

"It's okay. She's still potty training so we have to keep an eye out for those signs."

"Are we good?" Mallick asked me.

I nodded. "Thank you both. You don't know what this means to me."

"Thank us?" Lorraine said. "We're the ones who need to thank you."

Mallick snorted. "Do you have any idea how long this woman has been waiting for a grandpup?"

"And I can't imagine a more perfect one."

My phone rang and I gasped when I saw Vanessa's name pop up.

"Hello?"

"Hi Lucy. I was just checking to see if everything was okay and if Vada would be coming in today."

"What time is it?"

"A little after nine."

"Oh no. I'm so sorry. We were dealing with some family stuff," I decided was the best way to explain it. "And I just lost track of time. Is it okay if I bring her over now?"

"Sure, anytime. I heard about the incident over at the Shay's house and I just wanted to make sure everything was okay."

"Thanks for checking on us. She's fine. I'll have her there soon."

I hung up and sighed.

"Sorry, that was the school. Vada is late and it's after nine, so we are too. The clinic should have opened already."

"Are you working over at the clinic?" she asked.

"I am. I started last week."

"She's a healer, Lorraine. What better place for her to be?"

"A healer! After all you shared, you forgot to mention that little tidbit."

I blushed. "It's not something I really talk about."

"Well, you should. That's something to be proud of," she insisted.

"And it'll come in handy working with Micah," his father added.

"If you're taking Vada over to the school, and Micah needs to open the clinic, why don't I come with you."

"Oh, thanks, but you don't have to do that."

"Nonsense, I'd love to. Who do you have on your emergency contact list?"

"Huh?"

"For Vada's school. You had to have given them an emergency contact. I'm assuming that's Micah."

"Um, no, actually, I didn't know him when I signed her up. I actually met him because of it."

"What do you mean?" Mallick asked.

"The school required me to get a physical for her. I walked in and there he was."

"And how did you handle that, dear?"

I buried my face in my hands.

"She screamed 'no' at the top of her lungs and ran. Fortunately for me, she left her keys behind on the counter."

I nodded, still embarrassed by my first reaction.

"You weren't much better. You tried to leave the Pack."

"What?" Mallick barked. "Is this true?"

Micah glared at me but shrugged good naturedly.

"I thought she was already mated and upset that I even felt the call. I mean, come on, she had a small child."

"You assumed there had to be a father."

"Basically."

"Did you go to Kyle?"

"I did and he denied my request and then explained her situation. I wasn't supposed to say or do anything, so of course I left there and drove straight to her house to confront her. I don't think Kyle knows about that part so let's keep it in the family."

Family. It truly felt like I was a part of a family now.

"Well come, let's get this sweet girl to school," Lorraine said, picking up Vada and carrying her towards the front door.

"And I'll swing by and help open the clinic with you," Mallick told Micah.

Lorraine took control and carried Vada to the car and then strapped her in. I didn't even know what to do with myself.

"Do you need a ride to the clinic?" I asked Micah.

He pulled me into his arms and kissed me right there in front of the house he grew up in for the whole world to see.

"We'll walk. I'll see you when you get back."

He let me go and then leaned into the car and kissed Vada on the head. "You be good at school today."

"Okay," she promised.

My heart swelled as I watched them.

"That is the look of a woman in love with her mate," Lorraine said as I watched father and son walk away.

"That obvious?"

"Nothing makes a mother's heart happier than seeing her pup find his mate and fall in love. Someday, you'll see."

We got into the car, and I made the short drive over to the school.

"Now, if Micah isn't your emergency contact, who is?" she asked.

"Um, Kelsey, I think. I didn't really have anyone else to put down."

"Well, you do now. We should get it sorted while we're here. Micah should definitely be your next in line for emergencies, but if you'll allow it, I'd like to be on there too. In fact, if you'll approve it, I'd love to be on her approved pick-up list as well. That way if you ever need me, it's all set."

"Okay," I agreed before I could chicken out and overthink it.

"Alright. And don't worry about a thing. I'll order a car seat today and pick up a few things to keep at the house. I do hope you'll bring this sweet girl by often. How about dinner tonight since we never really got around to breakfast this morning."

"Um, tonight?" I took a deep breath. *It's okay to put boundaries in place,* I reminded myself. "Honestly, I think tomorrow would be better, if that's okay. We've had a really crazy few days and a quiet night at home is just what we need tonight."

She smiled at me and nodded as she reached over and squeezed my arm.

"Right answer. Not that that was a test or anything, because I selfishly would love to have you all over tonight. But this is your family, and you have to first and foremost do what's best for the three of you. It won't stop me from asking for more than I deserve, but never cower or be afraid to say no."

I laughed, feeling like I had a new ally in my court.

"Well then, no. Not to tonight."

"Tomorrow?"

Grinning, I nodded. "Tomorrow."

Micah

Chapter 18

People had been waiting outside the clinic when I arrived, and a steady stream kept coming throughout the day. Mostly just cuts and scrapes, minor injuries from the mudslides.

Dad had stuck around through the morning, lending a hand. It was nice to have him back in the office, though I didn't want him making a habit of it.

I felt like I'd barely seen Lucy because we were so busy. So much so that when she left to go pick up Vada, I didn't even notice until the toddler escaped and launched into my arms as she ran down the hall trying to get away from her mother.

Snatching her out of thin air, I cradled her to my chest as I walked my patient to the front door.

"Vada," Lucy warned.

"She's okay," I assured her taking a moment to pull her into my arms and relishing in the comfort that came from being surrounded by my two favorite ladies. "With any luck this stream of patients will slow soon."

"No such luck. Nonna's back in room three."

She handed me her file.

I groaned, knowing damn well there wasn't a thing wrong with that woman. She just wanted to pick my brain for a firsthand account of what happened out at the caves.

"I'm on it," I told her turning and heading for the office.

"Hey. Baby," she said, holding out her hands expectantly.

"I a big girl, Doc."

"Yes, you are. And my wingman for this appointment."

"Give me my kid back."

"No way. I need her right now. Plus, she's mine too," I insisted.

Before she could protest further, I turned and ran down the hall bouncing Vada on my hip and making her laugh.

I straightened when we reached the room and walked in with a straight face.

"Nonna, I'm surprised to see you back in here so soon. What's going on today?"

Her face lit up when she saw Vada.

Yeah, she wasn't fooling me.

"Is this Lucy's daughter?"

"Yes Ma'am. This is Vada."

"Vada? What a unique name."

"Don't even try it. I know you. You've already gotten all the gossip you can about my mate and Miss Vada here."

She smiled slyly before reaching out and taking the baby from me.

"You're mate, huh?"

"You heard me."

"Does your mother know?"

"She does. She met them this morning. Is that why you're here?"

Nonna seemed genuinely surprised.

"I hadn't heard. I'm glad though. Lorraine has always wanted to be a grandmother."

"I yike Grandma Doc," Vada told her.

"Grandma Doc?"

"My mother."

"Isn't that adorable." She gushed over the baby a little longer.

"Nonna, do you want to tell me why you're here?"

"Well, I have this pain in my shoulder. I'm sure you've seen a lot of that sort of thing, what with the mudslide yesterday and all. I'm actually surprised to see you here. I heard you were hurt pretty badly in that accident."

And there it was. Sly old gal. It was really no wonder she had adopted an entire family of foxes.

"I'm fine," I assured her.

"And Lucy, your mate, she's the one that saved you, right?"

"She did."

"A healer. How wonderful!"

I neither confirmed nor denied her claim.

"Will she be assisting more with patients now?"

"Lucy has a job," I reminded her.

"You're not going to give me even a small tidbit, are you?"

"Which shoulder has been bothering you?" I asked.

"Oh fiddle. I don't remember. Can't you just give an old lady a nibble?"

"This is not gossip central. Go hang out at the Crate if you want the latest gossip."

She looked stunned by my statement.

"I do not go to the Crate to seek gossip. I go there to spread it," she informed me.

I laughed. "You're not getting anything from me. Patient doctor confidentiality. How many times do I have to remind you of that?"

"It doesn't count when you're both."

I snorted. "Nonna, it's been a really long day and even longer weekend. I'm exhausted. Do you actually want me to look at that shoulder."

"No, I'm fine for now. If it keeps acting up, I'll be back."

She winked at me as she jumped off the table and left the room, taking my kid with her.

"Hey, you don't get to keep her!" I yelled after her.

Vada giggled and waved. "Bye, Doc."

"No, you don't, sweet girl," Lucy said snatching her from Nonna's arms.

Knowing everyone was where they should be, I sanitized the room to prepare for my next patient. Much to my relief, no more showed.

By four-thirty with no patients and the place cleaned and ready for a new day, I closed the clinic early.

"Are you sure?" Lucy asked.

"I'm exhausted and just want to go home."

She bit her lip and nodded.

"What?"

"I kind of liked having you stay over last night."

My wolf howled in my head in victory.

"So, um, are you talking about your home or mine?"

I pulled her into my arms and kissed her.

"Whichever you prefer."

She seemed torn.

"I really liked your place, but all of Vada's things are at mine."

"I'm not fixing that tonight, but if you and Vada want to move into my house, we can make that happen. And if you'd rather stay at the house you're in now, if that will be easier on her, then I'll talk to Kyle about purchasing it."

"Micah, you can't do that."

"The hell I can't. I don't care where we live, Luce. I just want to be with you and Vada."

She ran her hands through my hair and smiled.

"How did I get so lucky?"

"Funny. I'm pretty sure I'm the lucky one."

"For tonight, my house. But maybe this weekend we could start moving things over?" she asked, biting her lip and holding her breath for my response.

I kissed her. "I'll call in some favors to get some help."

"I really don't have much."

"Then it shouldn't take long to get you guys resettled."

A weight lifted from my shoulders knowing she had initiated this conversation. She wanted to be with me and that made me feel like the luckiest sonofabitch on the planet.

I really couldn't wait to fully merge our lives together and claim her once and for all.

*****

"I hungry," Vada protested on the drive home.

Lucy cringed. "I declined your mom's offer to go there for dinner tonight, told her we'd go tomorrow night. But I didn't go shopping or think about what we're having yet."

"I hungry!" Vada yelled again.

"Out or in?" I asked her.

"Huh?"

"Do you feel up to going out or would you prefer to stay in?"

She sighed. "I don't really care."

"Are you sure? I have plenty of food at my house and need to swing by and grab some clothes anyway. Or we can stop by the Silver Bells."

"What's Silver Bells?"

"It's like a 50's themed diner."

She considered that for a moment. "Yeah, that's fine," she conceded.

"What are you worried about?" I asked, sensing something was bothering her.

"It's nothing. It's fine."

"Lucy?"

She huffed. "I was just calculating cost in my head to make sure I can make it to payday."

I growled, making her eyes widen.

"You don't ever have to worry about that again."

"Micah, I'm a single mother. It's just life."

I growled again.

"You aren't single, and you aren't alone anymore."

It angered me to hear her even say that, though I tried to calm myself and my wolf down, knowing she hadn't meant it to come across quite like that.

I took a deep breath and let it out slowly.

"You're my mate. What's mine is yours and trust me, I have more than enough. I don't live extravagantly by any means, but if that's what you need, then we'll still be more than fine."

"I'm not a user, Micah. I'm not just going to mooch off of you or the Pack."

"Don't be so stubborn. It's my honor to care for you and Vada. Plus, you aren't *mooching*. You're working full time, investing in Pack resources, like sending Vada to preschool; it's not a handout, Luce. If we're truly moving forward with merging our lives together, then this is it. You and me, together. We're a team and that means what's mine is yours and what's yours is mine."

"You're getting the raw end of that deal," she muttered.

"No, I'm not. Because I get you and Vada. That's all I'll ever need."

She reached over and took my hand, but I didn't miss the way she tried to wipe her cheek without me noticing.

"Look," I said as I pulled in and parked in front of the restaurant. "You said you were ready to move forward by moving in with me. I have one stipulation."

"I'm listening."

"It's all or nothing, Luce. That means I'm adding you to my bank account so you do not ever have to worry about finances again. The house, the vehicles, all of it, in both our names. I'm asking for a full commitment. We may not have sealed our bond officially yet due to circumstances out of our control, but in my heart it's already a done deal."

"What do you get out of this deal?"

I side-eyed her. "Really?"

"I know, me and Vada, but really, Micah, I don't have much more than that to bring to the table here. It's not an equal balance."

"You're my mate, Lucy. None of that matters."

"I was raised to pull my own weight. I know it's just me being prideful, but I want to be equal partners with you in life. Equal. Can you understand that?"

"Okay," I said. "You want to contribute something more. I can respect that. But remember, I wasn't going to bring this up, not yet, but you asked what you can contribute. There's one thing I want more than anything and only you can give it to me."

I could see her wracking her brain trying to think of something.

"What? I don't have anything."

"You have everything," I insisted.

"So what is it you want more than anything?"

I turned and really looked at her. I needed her to know just how serious I was.

"Once we're fully mated, I want to legally adopt Vada. That's something only you can give me, Lucy."

This time I was the one nervously waiting on her response.

When she didn't answer right away, I started talking more.

"Just hear me out. It makes sense. It will secure her future. If, God forbid, anything happens to you before our bond is fully sealed, she'll be protected. I mean, it's not like I wouldn't do that anyway, but I mean legally protected. In my heart, she's as much mine as you are."

She stared at me on the verge of hyperventilating.

"You're serious? You want to adopt my daughter?"

"Yes," I blurted out and then reconsidered when she burst into tears.

I pulled her into my arms feeling so helpless. I didn't know what to do.

"You want to claim Vada, too?"

"Of course I do. I'm the only father she's ever going to know."

Lucy sobbed in my arms as I held her.

"I'm sorry. I didn't think you'd be so shocked or upset by it. You don't have to make a decision right this second. Just please, think about it?"

Lucy

Chapter 19

He wasn't understanding. I could hear the pain in his voice and that was the last thing I wanted.

I looked up to smile at him. He was so handsome, successful, kind, giving, so much more than I deserved, but selfishly, I wanted it all. This was my chance at a true happily ever after.

Micah had already proven to me how he would be there for me and my daughter. I knew he cared about Vada, and I was pretty sure that her unique start to life wasn't an issue for him, but adoption? He wanted to adopt her?

I leaned over and kissed him, smiling against his lips.

"I'm all in," I whispered confidently.

He jerked back to look at me.

"You mean it?"

"You have no idea how much that would mean to me," I whispered.

"Wait, you're okay with it? Because I thought maybe you were freaked out by me asking."

I shook my head.

"Just overwhelmed," I confessed. "I never even let myself think for a second that this could be my life, that you'd want both of us as much as we need you."

"I don't just want you both, I desperately need you, and I desperately need her, too. You're a package deal and I'm the lucky man who gets to call you both mine."

I hugged him as I cried some more.

This man was everything I never allowed myself to dream of.

"I hungry!" Vada protested loudly from the backseat.

He chuckled. "We know."

"Why Mommy crying Doc?"

"I think she's just happy."

I nodded. "So happy."

He kissed me once more and then searched around until he found some spare napkins in the glove box and handed me one.

"I must look like a complete mess. Maybe this isn't such a good idea tonight."

"You look beautiful, and I think it's a perfect idea. We have much to celebrate. And no stressing about money."

"I promise not to say a word."

He got out of the car and retrieved Vada from her seat and then walked around and helped me out. I was a hot mess with red puffy eyes that clearly showed I'd been crying, but I was beaming inside on the verge of overflowing with happiness.

"Hey Doc," a beautiful silver haired woman with stunning mismatched eyes greeted us. "How many?"

"Just me and my girls tonight," he said proudly.

"Do you need a highchair for her?"

"That would great," he said, answering for me.

"Nonna told me congratulations are in order. Hi, I'm Sapphire," the woman told me when we reached our seats.

"Lucy."

"I think you know my sister, Susan?"

"Susan's your sister?" I blurted out. The two looked nothing alike.

She laughed. "Yes, she is. She's the best."

"She really is," I agreed.

"Do you guys need a minute to look over the menu or do you know what you want?"

"How about drinks? I'm just going to have water," Micah said.

"Predictable," Sapphire teased. "How about you, Lucy?"

"Water's fine," I said matching his order.

"She'll have tea," Micah corrected.

Sapphire looked at me as I rolled my eyes at him.

"Tea would be great."

"You got it. And the little one?"

"Milk?"

Micah cringed.

"Bad for the tummy?" I asked.

"Yeah. It might be a little heavy on her. How about some apple juice and a water so we can dilute it for her. She got into a bit too much candy last night and so we're easing back into food and all."

"Well, she's lucky to have full access to you, then," she said as she laid a hand on his shoulder.

A growl erupted from me before I could stop it even though I knew she was just being friendly.

Micah bit back a grin.

"Still mating, then? Got it. Hands off. I'll be right back with your drinks."

"I'm so sorry."

"You have nothing to apologize for. You're a lucky woman."

"I know," I said, watching my mate find humor in my slip up.

"Thanks, Sapphire," he said before turning his full attention back to me. "I didn't overstep with the drink thing, did I?"

I shook my head. "Not at all. You're right. I just wasn't thinking."

"You know, I fully respect that you are her mother and I'm just grateful to be a part of your lives…"

I shook my head, cutting him off right there.

"No. We agreed. All in. You're right. You are going to be the only father she ever has. I can't say it'll always be easy because I'm not used to having someone else to share the burdens of parenthood with, and I can't even promise we'll always agree on things where she's concerned, but I'm going to try."

I reached across the table and took his hands in mine.

"Hungry, Doc."

"Sorry sweet pea. Here comes Sapphire with our drinks and we'll get your order in right away."

I looked over the menu unsure of what would be good for her on a mostly empty stomach. When I'd gone to pick her up Vanessa had warned me that she hadn't really eaten much for lunch. The fact that she seemed to be starving now was probably a good sign.

"What are you having?" I asked.

"Beef tips over mashed potatoes and some green beans."

"I not yike green beans," Vada said scrunching up her nose.

I sighed. "We're still working on vegetables. She can be stubborn."

"How about mashed potatoes?"

"I yike dem."

Her little cherub face lit up in excitement.

"They have grilled chicken nuggets on the kid's meal that probably wouldn't be too hard on her stomach."

"Okay," I quickly agreed, finding myself relieved not to have to make that decision for once.

Sapphire set down our drinks and Micah immediately reached for Vada's sippy cup to pour a bit of juice into it and then top the rest off with water.

"Oh," I said catching Sapphire watching me watch him as she waited for my order. "She'll have the kid's grilled chicken nuggets and a side of mashed potatoes."

"Gravy?"

"No," Micah and I said at the same time.

I laughed. “And I’ll have the chicken pot pie special.”

“Great. Be right out shortly.”

She disappeared without any further growling incidents.

The food came and it was really good. Most importantly, Vada devoured hers, then somehow Micah convinced her to try a green bean. Much to my shock, she ate two of them off his plate.

“See, not so bad, huh?”

“It okay,” she conceded happily accepting another spoonful of his mashed potatoes in reward.

Feeling more relaxed than I should be and happier than I could ever remember, Micah paid the bill, snatched up Vada, and escorted me back to the car to drive us home.

“Are you okay if I swing by my place to grab a bag?”

“Of course,” I said.

I wasn’t sure why I was nervous about him sleeping over again. It’s not like he hadn’t already. Somehow this time felt different, though. This felt like the start of something more as we talked about truly blending our lives together.

Plus, there was that issue where we’d almost bonded but haven’t yet.

I yawned, feeling exhausted as the last few days crashed in on me.

“I’ll be quick.”

He leaned over and kissed me, making Vada giggle in the backseat.

“Was that funny?” I asked her when he was gone.

“Doc kiss Mommy.”

I didn’t how to respond to that or how to explain everything going on to my two-year-old daughter.

“Mommy, pee.”

“Now?”

“Uh-huh.”

“Okay, hold on.”

I jumped out of the car and opened the back door to quickly remove her from her car seat.

"Hold on. We're going to make it."

I didn't know how much time we had. Sometimes she still waited until the last second to tell me when she had to go.

I burst through Micah's door and made a mad dash for the nearest bathroom.

Vada's eyes widened.

"Dis smell yike Doc."

"This is Doc's house," I told her. "Do you like the smell?"

She smiled and nodded her head.

"I yike Doc."

"I know you do. How would you feel about living here?"

"Wif Doc?"

"Yes."

She seemed to consider it for a moment. I tried not to grin at the serious look on her face but also wondered if maybe she was doing a little more than just peeing.

"Okay," she finally said as she wiped herself, and jumped down like a big girl.

While I was flushing the toilet, she ran out of the bathroom.

"Vada!" I hollered.

Micah peeked his head in.

"Everything okay?"

"Vada had to use the bathroom and now she's loose in your house."

"Doc!" we heard her yell.

"Where'd you go, sweetie?"

"Here."

He chuckled but followed the sound of her voice to find her standing in the middle of the hallway.

"Wut room mine?"

"Huh?"

"Mommy say we move here wif you."

"She told you that?"

She nodded as I stood back and watched, wondering how he'd react to her proclamation.

He swooped her up into his arms and proceeded to show her each of the bedrooms.

"So, you can't have mine and Mommy's room which is this one," he said showing her the room. "But any other room can be yours. Which would you like?"

"Dis one," she said without hesitation pointing to the room closest to the master bedroom.

"Done," he assured her. "We need to move out this stuff and make room for your things, huh?"

"Uh-huh. Dat Vada room now."

My eyes misted over. This was really happening.

Later that evening while Micah settled Vada in for the night, insisting I rest up, I couldn't help but start to imagine what life could be like for us with Micah playing a big role in it.

The future had always terrified me, but now, it didn't look so dark, or lonely. Vada was thriving here, and no one really seemed to think anything of her unique situation. They treated her like a normal, healthy kid. It was more than I ever allowed myself to believe possible.

"Is she down?"

"She is. You look exhausted. Ready for bed?"

"Is that a loaded question?" I asked, letting him pull me to my feet.

"I promise to behave and let you sleep… for tonight at least."

"How did I get so lucky?"

"Pretty sure, I'm the lucky one, babe."

Micah

Chapter 20

The day flew by. Things were still busy, but not nearly as bad. Despite the craziness of the weekend, since Lucy and I had made a verbal commitment to each other, things were quickly falling back into step.

We made a great team. Her organizational skills were every bit as tight as mine. She was the perfect woman by my side and not just in my personal life.

Still, I didn't want to push her too hard, too fast, but when I got slammed just before closing with a gnash to the head and an infected splinter, I broke down and asked for help.

"Look, I don't know how you'll feel about this, but if we're going to make it to my parents' house on time for dinner, I could really use your help."

"Sure, what it is?"

"Any chance you'd be up for healing that head wound while I tackle the splinter?"

She froze and her eyes widened.

"If you're not comfortable actually healing it, that's okay, just bandage and send him on his way. It's just a surface wound, but you know how head wounds bleed like a sonofabitch."

I thought she was going to turn me down, but much to my surprise, she agreed.

Knowing she would be worried about Vada being left alone, I snatched her up and took her with me.

"Who do we have here?" Sally cooed.

"This is Vada, my daughter," I told her, proudly claiming the child.

"Hi Vada."

"Hi," she said without hesitation.

When Sally reached for her, Vada happily went to her.

If I didn't know her background, I'd never suspect the trauma my baby girl had suffered. Sure, there were moments that struck as painful reminders, but for the most part she was open and loving, easily receptive to others. She was amazing.

While Vada kept her distracted, I quickly worked to remove the splinter.

"Ow." Sally jerked as I squeezed the infection from her.

"Boo-boo?" Vada asked. "I fix."

Before I could stop her, Vada reached over and grabbed Sally's finger then giggled.

"All better."

When she pulled her tiny hand away, I saw she was right.

My jaw dropped.

"Did you see that?" Sally asked. "It doesn't hurt at all. Thank you, Vada."

While my patient marveled over her unexpected healing, I just stared at my daughter in shock.

Pulling it together long enough to get Sally out of there, I waited out in the main area for Lucy to finish.

"I'm glad I could help," I heard her say as the teenage boy walked into the lobby and waved my way.

"Thanks Doc. Lucy did great, not even a scar," he praised.

"So you healed him?" I asked after he left.

She shrugged. "I think word's already out about me anyway. How'd the splinter go?"

"Um, it was interesting," I admitted, still trying to wrap my head around it. "You didn't mention to me that Vada is a healer as well."

"What are you talking about? She's two."

"Almost free," she reminded us.

"Sally's finger was infected, Luce. I removed the splinter, but the infection was still there. I was about to give her a salve and send her home when Vada grabbed it and suddenly there was no infection left. She healed her."

"Micah that's crazy. Vada is just a child. Most witches don't even show signs of powers this young, do they?"

"Honestly, I don't know. Kelsey supposedly had her powers at a very young age, but is that because she's an Alpha she-wolf or a witch?"

Lucy's eyes widened. "Kelsey's an Alpha?"

"Yeah. It's pretty much common knowledge around here. I believe that's why her bond sealed so quickly with Kyle and why she has to be super careful when doing big healings. Just like you can pull extra power from me, she will pull it from the entire Pack if she doesn't watch it."

"You had mentioned that a bit, but that's kind of scary, Micah."

"It's a gift, Luce, just like you, and apparently just like Vada."

She sighed and looked deflated.

"What's wrong?"

"As if she doesn't have enough against her, now this? You don't know what it's like to be different, to scare people."

I shook my head. "We'll protect her from that as best as we can. Setting up roots here will help. We're good with different around here."

I tried to smile reassuringly.

"Can we talk about it later? I think I need a little time for this to sink in. I mean she's always been a little different, but a healer? I never even saw that coming. How would I not know?"

"Give yourself a break, Luce. She's two."

I could tell she was thinking back through everything, trying to see what she'd missed and when.

"Come on, let's just walk over to Mom and Dad's. I think a bit of fresh air will do us all some good."

"Okay, let me grab the stroller out of the car."

"No. I big girl," Vada protested.

"I'll carry her if she gets tired of walking," I offered.

"Okay," Lucy conceded faster than I expected.

She was quiet on the walk. I probably shouldn't have thrown something so big at her like that. I had just assumed she knew and hadn't told me.

When we reached the house, she stopped and grabbed my arm. "Last year, shortly after we got back to New York to stay with my family, some of the neighborhood kids caught a rabbit in a trap. Vada and I stumbled across it out on a walk. She was very upset and helped me save the rabbit. I had thought I'd felt it injured and knew it would die, but by the time we released it, it was fine and hopped away like there was nothing wrong. Do you think that could have been Vada's doing?"

"I honestly don't know, but after what I just saw, it's possible."

Lucy sighed. "She talks to animals," she blurted out. "Or she thinks she does at least. I've always just blown it off, but now I can't help but wonder if that's possible too."

I pulled her into my arms and kissed her lightly at her temple.

"I don't know if that's possible or not. It's extremely rare for a witch to have more than one power. Kelsey is the only exception that I know of. But regardless of what her talents may be, the thing I know to be true is that she is an exceptional child and we're going to raise her like any normal kid while encouraging and appreciating whatever unique traits she may have."

"This really doesn't freak you out?"

"It really doesn't. So what if she's like you and can heal? It wouldn't bother me if we had a whole litter of pups just like you."

She sighed but didn't argue.

"I know life hasn't always been easy on you, Lucy, but from here on out, it's going to be better. I promise you that."

"Well, what are you three doing hanging around out here? Come on in, dinner's going to get cold," Mom fussed as she peeked her head out of the door to find us standing on the sidewalk talking.

I chuckled. "Yes, ma'am."

"Vada's here," she yelled into the house as she took her hand and walked her inside.

Within seconds, Dad had her in his arms.

"Wait until you see what Grandma Doc did today," he said conspiratorially.

"After dinner, Mallick," she scolded. "And it's like Grandpa Doc didn't have anything to do with it."

"What did you do?" I asked.

"Nothing any respectable grandparents wouldn't do," Mom insisted ushering us to the dining room where the table was already set with a feast.

"Mom?"

"Shh, now say grace and let's eat."

The food was delicious, and Lucy seemed genuinely happy to be there. She was relaxed, laughed, and talked with my parents. And when Mom insisted on fussing over Vada during dinner, Lucy didn't get so uptight and nervous about it.

"Vada, are you full, sweetie?" Dad asked.

"All done," she announced knowing she had everyone around the table enraptured by her.

Mom cleaned her up and Dad swooped in to snag her.

"Not yet," Mom insisted. "Show her the playroom first."

"Playroom?" I asked cautiously.

"Of course. She's our granddaughter. She needs toys and a place to sleep in case Lucy will let us have a sleepover sometime."

"Sleepover?" I questioned.

Hesitantly I got up and followed, taking Lucy's hand in mine and dragging her along with me.

"Should we be worried?" she whispered.

I nodded. "Definitely."

We heard Vada's squeal of delight before we reached the room that had previously been my childhood room.

I peeked inside and my jaw dropped.

The place was filled with toys. There was a kitchen set, a bookshelf filled with books, puzzles, and games. A twin sized bed with a slide and a fort beneath it filled part of the room.

The room had been painted a pale pink with flowers adorning the walls. I had no idea how I'd missed the smell of the fresh paint during dinner.

"I wuv it!" Vada announced as her new doting grandparents beamed with pride.

"Oh, that's not all," Dad insisted. "Come on, let's go out back."

"There's more?" Lucy asked.

I could feel her emotions well enough to know she was getting overwhelmed.

Outside in the backyard was now a playhouse with a carport housing a pink Jeep and a red motorcycle. There was a full swing set with a fort and rock wall that was nicer than the stuff they had at our local park.

On the deck next to his grill was a small plastic grill for Vada.

"How did you manage all of this in one day?" I blurted out as Vada ran around squealing, checking everything out.

"At the right price there's nothing I can't get done in a day," Mom confessed.

I groaned. "Mom, you can't spoil her like this."

"The hell I can't! That's a grandma's right."

Lucy had remained quiet, just standing there watching it all unravel. When I looked at her, I realized she was crying but had the biggest smile on her face.

When Mom noticed too, she walked over and hugged her.

"Thank you," Lucy whispered.

I knew it had nothing to do with the stuff they'd purchased. Their ridiculous over-the-top showing of how excited they were to welcome Vada into their lives showed by action far more than words could have ever portrayed.

I had told her life would be different here. I prayed this was only the start of keeping that promise.

A commotion inside the house put my wolf on edge, but instantly calmed as I turned and saw Grandpappy stumble out onto the deck. His balance wasn't very good these days.

"Marshal, what are you doing here?" Mom asked. "You're late for dinner, but I can fix you up a plate if you'd like."

"Came to meet my great-grandpup," he announced.

I grinned. "Grandpappy, this is Lucy, my mate."

"Lucy? Nice to meet you. Where's my little Vada?"

"She's serving tea to Mallick in her new playhouse."

"Lucy, it's nice to meet you. We've waited a long time for this bozo to settle down."

I groaned. "Grandpappy, I'm not that old."

"Hogwash. Who ever heard of a pup waiting till his thirties to settle down and start a family?"

"The kind who's been patiently waiting to cross paths with his one true mate."

The man's eyes sparkled. "Good answer. My Tabby is the love of my life and my true mate, you know. And your parents are true mates too."

"So why would you expect anything less of me?"

He just grinned. "You've done well, Micah."

It was the same old story I'd heard a million times. As the only child of an only child, following in both my dad and grandpappy's footsteps, there had always been a lot of expectations put on me. I had never minded it, but I was not about to compromise on a mate just to give them a grandpup.

I had never doubted for a second that they wouldn't take Vada and Lucy into the family, but even I was not prepared for the level of insanity my parents were bestowing on them.

Watching them all, I couldn't help but wish Nanny was there to see it too. I missed her. We all did.

As the evening started to settle, we moved back inside. I was talking with Mom and Lucy in the living room when Dad walked in looking confused.

"Where'd Dad and Vada go?"

"What do you mean?" Lucy asked. "They're in the playroom."

"No, they're not," he said.

My wolf immediately surfaced with a growl as I jumped and ran to find my daughter.

"He's growing quite protective of her," my mother observed.

"That's not a bad thing. He's the only father she'll ever have," Lucy explained.

"And a damn good one, too," Dad said proudly.

"Where the hell would he take her?" I asked calling forward my wolf nose as I started tracking them.

Lucy was starting to panic.

"They aren't in the house?" she yelled after me as I stood on the front porch trying to get my bearings straight.

"This way," I finally said.

The three of them followed closely behind me. A block away, Dad groaned.

"Come on. I know where they're headed."

"The nursing home?" Mom guessed.

"That would be my guess," he admitted.

Sure enough, their combined scent led me in that direction and just before the building came into view, I saw him walking slightly hunched to one side while holding her little hand. The two of them made quite the odd pair.

"Grandpappy!" I yelled as they stopped and turned to me.

"Doc!" Vada smiled and waved.

Lucy ran ahead and grabbed her up in her arms.

"Are you okay? You scared us. You can't just leave without telling Mommy."

"Sorry. Grandpappy Doc take me to see Nanny Doc."

"Nanny Doc?"

"Tabitha, my mate."

"Oh," Lucy said, and I knew from the tone of her voice that she had thought my grandmother was dead.

Truth be told, sometimes it was easier to believe she was.

Six years ago, Nanny had taken a fall, causing severe head trauma. Even her wolf hadn't been able to heal her. In fact, to the best of my knowledge, she'd never even been able to shift and try. She didn't talk and barely acknowledged us, but in her eyes, I could still see her trapped inside her own body. It made it all the harder to watch as her aging body decayed at an alarming rate.

The hardest part of all was knowing that when her time ended, she would take Grandpappy away with her. It was like a double-edged sword, wanting to end her suffering while knowing how much life and energy was still left in him.

"Are you okay with this?" I whispered to Lucy. "She's not well."

I tried to explain without using the words and hoping she understood me. Seeing my Nanny wasn't easy on any of us, but my concern was more for Vada. She was just an innocent child and while I suspected she'd seen death firsthand before, I didn't want to subject her further.

"It clearly means a lot to him. It's fine," she assured me.

"Come on Vada, let's go see Nanny Doc," Grandpappy announced as he took her hand in his and continued on their adventure.

Lucy

Chapter 21

From the way they had mentioned her, I honestly thought the woman was dead. My wolf was still on edge from the adrenaline rush of finding my daughter missing,

Vada was okay though and in a weird way it was sweet that the old man wanted to show her off as his own.

Having a real family was going to take some getting used to.

Lorraine and Mallick had gone way overboard for Vada at their house. I still couldn't believe they had managed to buy and setup all of that stuff in just a day. It was insane and far more than I would have done for her myself.

After time with the Raglan, things didn't seem quite so important to me. People mattered more. It was why it had been so devasting when my own family had rejected us the way they had.

Micah's family wasn't them, though. I was going to have to constantly remind myself of that, but it was true. I appreciated the efforts they were going to more than I could ever put into words, even if it was a lot.

Micah and I followed Grandpappy into the nursing home. He waved a few people along the way and stopped to introduce Vada to the nurses at one of the stations. It was cute how they all fussed at her.

I reached for Micah's hand for support. Everything inside of me screamed to grab my daughter and run back to the safety of our house where I could protect her from the idiocy of others.

"Breathe, Luce," he whispered.

I hadn't realized I was holding my breath, just waiting for someone to say something about my kid.

Our fresh start here in San Marco was still haunted by events of my past. I kept waiting for everyone to somehow find out about us and what we had been through and have this whole illusion come crashing down on me.

Most of the time those fears were laid to rest, but my anxiety spiked with unfounded fears every single time we entered a new situation, and I certainly hadn't been prepared for this one.

His thumb drew small soothing circles on the back of my hand. That simple little gesture helped center me. With a deep soothing breath to steady my shallow breathing, I managed to smile and nod appropriately as Mallick introduced me to a few of the staff there.

"We'll hang back here. Why don't you and Micah go with Marshal to meet Tabitha," Lorraine suggested.

The old man turned back toward us as if he had forgotten we were even there, but his whole face lit up at the mention of his mate.

Silently we followed him down the hall and into a small room.

"Tabby, I brought you a new friend to meet. This is Vada," he told her, but the woman didn't move. The only sign of life was the way her eyes cut towards his voice.

Still, he approached her taking a moment to wrap his arms around her and kiss her forehead.

"Vada is Micah's pup. This is her mother, Lucy. They haven't bonded yet, but it's only a matter of time. She's his true mate," he explained, filling in the silence of the room.

Tears pricked my eyes as I watched him interact with her. The love between them was tangible.

Micah led me over to an open chair. He sat down and pulled me onto his lap as he wrapped his arms around my waist.

"Nanny, this is Lucy, my mate, and our daughter, Vada."

The way his possessively claimed her, nearly broke me as fresh tears glistened in my eyes.

"Hi," I managed to squeak out through the lump of emotions in my throat.

"I Vada. I two but almost free," she told the woman talking to her much in the same way Marshal had.

A small smile tipped the corners of the woman's lips as her eyes found Vada's.

When Marshal sat down next to her and took her hand, Vada reached for her other and then she started to cry.

My heart dropped as I moved quickly to her side.

"What's wrong, sweetie?"

"She's trapped, mommy," Vada cried. "Help."

I pulled her into my arms as she cried.

"I wish I could, baby."

"No. Help," she demanded as she grabbed my hands and laid them on Tabitha's. "Fix!"

I looked up to Marshal's face as he watched us and saw fresh hope in his eyes.

A terrible feeling settled into my gut.

Turning around I sought help from Micah.

"The damage was severe," he explained. "A fall that caused severe head trauma. We've done everything possible to keep her comfortable and well cared for."

"Her wolf couldn't heal her?"

He shook his head. "I'm not sure if it caused damage to her wolf or just a disconnect. Grandpappy swears he can still feel her inside, and they can talk a little through their bonded connection, but not much. As far as I know she hasn't been able to shift since the accident."

"Mommy, fix," Vada demanded again.

"I'm not sure mommy can do anything to help. When was the fall?" I asked.

"Six years ago."

I nodded sadly. I didn't think there was anything I could do, but Vada's insistence didn't stop as she grabbed my hands and placed one on each side of Tabitha's face.

A shock ran through me as I gasped.

"Lucy!" Micah yelled in the distance, but it was too late.

The room around me faded away as I found myself lost in a different sort of darkness. It wasn't uncommon for me to see inside a person during a healing. I don't know if sight was exactly the right word though. It wasn't like I had x-ray vision or anything. It was a different sort of vision filled with contrasting dark and light.

In this moment I was trapped in pure darkness. I could feel goosebumps break out across my skin and a warm hand comfort me.

Up ahead, just out of reach was a tiny dot of light. In my mind, I moved towards it. The closer I got, the brighter the light became until I was surrounded by it, looking out into the darkness.

Trapped had been a good word. This woman was literally trapped inside her own mind and body. I had no idea how long I was there. Time lost all meaning.

It was as if I could see her memories, experience her life as I sifted through it all.

The day she met Marshal.

Mallick's birth.

The stress and love of watching her son grow up.

Becoming a grandmother. The joy of that moment was overwhelming.

The images kept coming, sad ones, happy ones, scary ones. I could see it all, the full journey this woman's life had taken, and then it just stopped.

None of this was anything like I'd ever experienced before. I'd healed numerous people, but not like this. Bones, muscles, physical injuries were easy, this was something entirely different.

It felt as if I sat there staring back at her past, with nothing but darkness ahead of me. The synapses of her brain were broken. I could see the point of break similar to a broken bone, but I didn't know how to fix it.

I reached out to touch it as I would an injury, but hot pain shot through my body and I heard screaming in the distance.

Vaguely aware of Micah's presence, I felt him pull me back, but I fought against it, instead pulling from the power of our bond. It boosted my strength, but I knew instantly it wasn't going to be enough.

"No!" I yelled as I touched the break once more. I had to try.

"I help!" I heard a sweet voice in the distance and then felt a new presence--Vada.

Her hands were on mine causing an intense jolt of electricity to run through me. I channeled that energy to the break point and was thrown back with the power of it.

Strong arms wrapped around me as I sank back into darkness.

****

When I came to, I was first aware of the laughter around me. Slowly my eyes opened to show I was lying in a bed in a small room surrounded by people. Micah was sitting next to me, my head in his lap.

"Vada?" I asked.

"I here mommy."

Her sweet little hand clasped mine.

"We did it."

"What?"

"You did it, Luce. You healed my nanny."

I tried to sit up, but my head was pounding, and I quickly closed my eyes again.

"Take it easy. You've been out for a few hours."

"I have?"

"Yeah. Kelsey stopped by and checked on you. She said there was nothing wrong. You were just exhausted. It's kind of a miracle. I had no idea you could do something like this."

"What did I do?" I asked, confused.

"You healed me," an old woman said.

"You gave me back my Tabby," Marshal added.

"She was able to shift afterwards and complete the healing. It's unbelievable. If I wasn't here to see it with my own eyes, I never would have believed it," Micah praised.

"I hadn't been able to shift in over six years. Lord knows I tried. I was right here all along," she insisted.

My eyes opened a little easier this time and I caught a glimpse of the love I'd so clearly felt as Marshal wrapped his arms around his mate, not even trying to hide the tears he shed.

"How are you feeling?" Micah asked me.

I took a second to do an internal assessment.

"I'm fine. A little tired, but otherwise okay."

"Why don't you get Lucy and Vada home," Lorraine suggested. "It's late."

I looked up at him and he nodded.

"Are you up for walking?"

"I can grab a wheelchair," Mallick insisted.

"No need. I can carry her," Micah argued.

I snorted as I sat up slowly expecting to be dizzy or something, but I really did feel fine.

"I'm okay," I insisted.

Vada yawned as she hugged me.

"Good job, Mommy."

I kissed her, but let Micah lift her from me.

"Lucy," Tabitha said, reaching a hand out to me.

I took it and walked over to her. When I'd arrived, she had been nothing more than a shell of herself. Now, she looked vibrant and alive.

"I don't know how I'll ever thank you for this. You are truly an angel on Earth."

"I'm glad you're going to be okay," I told her, letting her hug me as I fought back against the emotional rollercoaster I was internally riding.

Before the others joined in, I motioned for Micah to get me out of there. I was still dealing with the emotional aftermath of such a personal healing.

People stopped and stared as we passed. Some whispered, many cried or waved. Word of what I had done was already spreading quickly.

I didn't say much on the ride back to my house. Vada fell asleep in her car seat, and I didn't protest when Micah parked and carefully lifted her into his arms. I relinquished control to him as he walked inside and put her to bed before returning to help me.

"It was her, you know? I was right there, and I tried working on it, but there was so much damage. When Vada jumped in, there was this indescribable jolt of energy that finished the healing, Micah. I've never experienced anything like it before, not even pulling from your energy through our bond. You were right. She's powerful."

"I know. But she's going to be okay because she has us. It might be a little more than potty training and learning to read, but we'll teach her what she needs to control it."

"It really doesn't bother you? We have no idea what her future will look like."

I didn't voice those fears often, but if I couldn't with my mate, then who could I? Suddenly it all felt like too much for just me to bear alone.

"Hey, that's our child and she's wonderful and unique. We will celebrate her differences and raise her in spite of them. We won't fail her."

I stared at him as tears burned my eyes.

"Our child?"

"Our child," he insisted. "I told you; I'm going to adopt her and make it official, but that piece of paper doesn't make her magically mine."

I nodded trying to stay strong while feeling overwhelmed with all that had happened today.

"I'm not sure what we did to deserve you," I teased.

His smile was slightly crooked as he shook his head.

"I'm the lucky one here."

He pulled me into his arms and kissed me, but then he frowned against my lips as he pulled back to look at me.

"I'm fine," I insisted feeling his worry.

"I know you, Luce. I can feel you. You aren't fine."

His words set a crack in the damn I'd been hiding behind and I couldn't stop the tears from falling. I incoherently tried to explain it all as he lifted me into his arms and carried me to bed.

Micah

Chapter 22

I didn't want to leave Lucy alone today to deal with everything that had happened, but she had stubbornly insisted. She got up and got Vada ready for school like it was any other day.

"Keeping a strict routine helps her, and me," she had insisted. "Plus, I have some work to finish up at the office and some errands to run. I'll be fine. You need to go about your day as usual. It's Wednesday, you hang out with Westin Force today, right?"

I had wanted to lie to her and tell her that only happened some of the time, but we were growing close quickly now and she would have known I was lying. So in the end I'd conceded and gone home to dress for the gym even though my heart, and my wolf, wanted to be with her instead.

As soon as I stepped into the gym, Silas threw a ball my way.

"You missed our run this morning," he said gruffly.

I scowled. I'd had a lot going on this morning and had struggled with leaving Lucy, but I wasn't about to admit that to him.

"Still hasn't sealed his bond," Grant said definitively. No doubt his wolf sensed it. "So don't go too hard on him."

"Why the hell not?" Baine asked.

I just groaned in response.

"Is she fighting it?" Tarron asked, sounding concerned.

"No. It's not that. We just haven't found the time."

"Again, sorry about that, man," Ben added.

"That wasn't your fault."

"Kind of was. That was my candy stash the kids got into."

"What the hell? You aren't supposed to be eating a bunch of sugary crap like that," Painter reminded him.

Ben just rolled his eyes making me laugh.

"Well, I heard a rumor this morning that Lucy healed your grandmother. Is that true?" Silas asked.

"Tabitha is healed?" Grant asked. "How is that even possible?"

I smiled. "She is. She's alert and well. In fact, she's moving out of the nursing home today."

"A complete healing from years of head trauma?" he questioned.

I nodded. "Yeah. She described it as being trapped in her own body. Her mind is as sharp as ever. Dad and Grandpappy are keeping a close eye on her, but she's going to be okay."

"That's really amazing, man."

"Thanks."

"And Kelsey couldn't have done this?" Silas questioned.

I shrugged. "To be honest, none of us really considered using their healing powers in this way. I guess we all just assumed with brain damage that it couldn't happen, or maybe we just considered it too far gone for a healing. I don't know. This certainly could open new doors for us now. I haven't really stopped to consider it yet."

I knew I had a few other patients suffering similarly, but I didn't want everyone to get their hopes up that Lucy was suddenly a miracle worker. We both knew that Vada had played a significant role in healing Nanny, and there was no way in hell I was I going to exploit her for that. I didn't have to talk to Lucy about it to know that we were both on the same page when it came to that. Vada should be allowed as normal a childhood as possible. What she chose to do with her powers as an adult would be up to her. Until then, I would do whatever I could to shield her from the world of curiosity who would use her for her gifts.

"Well, I'm happy for you and your family. Tabitha was a remarkable woman and it killed me to see her like that," Grant admitted.

"I know man. We all felt the same. It's pretty surreal right now. I was right there to witness it and I can still hardly believe it."

Jake ran into the gym taking the heat off of me.

Silas scowled. "Where the hell have you been?"

He sighed, looking a little defeated. "Sorry. Family crisis this morning."

Silas just glared at him raising one eyebrow higher than the other and causing Jake to crack under the silent scrutiny.

"Charlie hitched a ride in my bag this morning. I swear I didn't know she was there."

"What do you mean hitched a ride?" Silas demanded.

"Exactly as it sounds. She's such a small little mouse. I didn't even see her, but she hid in my bag and then escaped in headquarters while we were out on our run. Apparently, she was going through some of Martin's files in the data center when Archie busted her. It led to a full-on chase and let's just say he is not happy about it."

"Why didn't we get called in?" he grumbled.

"Because Delta did. Michael and his team is not happy about it. Rumor has it Linc went off on her when he finally caught her, and she bit him." Jake groaned.

"Linc went off on someone? I didn't even know he had it in him," Baine teased.

"Apparently there's a bit of a bomb inside that guy when pushed to his limits, which Charlie did. Anyway, Archie banned her from the premises, and I had to take her home. Alaina acted like it was our fault for traumatizing that stupid mouse."

"Stupid is not the world I'd use for Charlie," Tarron said with a laugh. "More like evil genius."

Jake sighed as I laughed.

"Never a dull moment around here," I pointed out.

"Crisis over?" Painter asked.

"Yeah. For now."

"Great, then let's play some ball."

"Hey, I have a favor to ask you guys," I blurted out.

"And then we can actually play?" Baine teased.

"What is it?" Silas asked.

"If you guys are free this weekend, do you think you could help move Lucy and Vada over to my house? I'd like to paint the spare room for Vada as well."

"So you haven't bonded with her, but you're moving in together?" Grant teased.

"We'll get around to that part and living together will help with that. I hope," I confessed making the others laugh.

"Of course we will," Jake said. "I'm really happy for you, man."

"Thanks."

"We'll all be there. My orders," Silas barked.

"Yes, sir," Baine said while saluting dramatically.

"We'll be there," Taylor assured me. She couldn't stop grinning.

"Don't make a big deal out of this," I warned her.

"Wouldn't dream of it."

Grant laughed wrapping his arms around his mate and kissing her bare shoulder in a rare showing of open affection while on the clock. Working together, they had an unspoken hands-off rule during work hours, though even I knew that was only for the team's benefit. There had been plenty of rumors of catching the two of them in compromising positions in closets and behind locked doors, but they did at least try to keep their hands to themselves for the most part.

"That means T's about to pull in the mates as well. They'll have your bachelor pad properly girly-fied before the weekend's over," Baine assured me.

I groaned but couldn't stop grinning.

"Oh, he's a goner already. Doesn't even care one bit."

I shrugged. "If Lucy wants flowers and shit all over the house, so be it. I don't care as long as I have her and Vada with me."

Baine rolled his eyes dramatically. "Spoken like a truly whipped male."

"Can you pansies just shut up and play some basketball already?" Silas grumbled.

Getting lost in the game was just what I needed to clear my head. This time I was far more focused and put up a good fight even if my team did fall short by two points.

"Rematch," I demanded. "That was a foul, and you know it."

Baine just smirked and shrugged. "All's fair in love and basketball."

"That's a stupid thing to say. There are rules for a reason," Tarron reminded him. "And Micah's right. You cheated."

"Did he?" Silas challenged.

I snorted, knowing we weren't going to win this one.

"You're only agreeing because he was on your team," I said with a laugh.

"Better luck next time," Silas told me while barking for the team to hit the showers.

That was my cue to leave. I'd head home and shower there instead.

"Hey, are we still on for D&D tonight at your place?" Tarron asked.

"Yeah, of course. Why wouldn't be?"

"Well with everything going on with your grandmother, Lucy, and all, I just wanted to make sure."

"See you tonight," I simply said as I left them to drive home, shower, and prepare for the evening.

Lucy called me as I was setting up the last of the table for the game.

"Hey. I missed you today," I said as I answered the phone.

"Missed you too. Vada called asking about babysitting tonight."

It made me uncomfortable letting others watch our girl, but I had loved having Lucy at D&D night and selfishly wanted her here tonight.

"What did you tell her?"

"Just that I would call her back when I knew what I was doing."

I sighed, hoping she wouldn't hear it.

"If you don't want to come for game night, it's okay. I'll just come by afterwards."

"Oh, okay," she said weirdly.

I knew something was off.

"Luce."

"Yeah?"

"I want you here," I blurted out. "Unless you really didn't enjoy it. I loved having you here."

"Really?"

"Of course. Vada and Silas can handle babysitting for a few hours, or you can just bring her with you. Starting next week when we play here, they're going to have to get used to having our girl around anyway. Or we could let Mom and Dad watch her instead."

"That's probably too much to ask of them."

I laughed. "Did you see the room they created for her? Trust me, they'll want to do this."

"We'll see. I guess I'll let Vada and Silas have another go at it for tonight. I mean, they did keep her alive last week."

We both laughed remembering the disturbing text updates Silas kept sending.

"You're sure?"

"Yeah, it'll be fine. Plus, it was really weird not seeing you today. I didn't particularly like it. And I had no idea what to do with myself all day while you and Vada were gone."

"Maybe you and Kelsey could get together for lunch or something next week."

"What did you do all day?"

I snorted. "Nothing you'd want a part of. I get together with Bravo team at the gym on Wednesdays. I work out with them and then spend the afternoon playing basketball, at least when they're not out of town on a mission. It's just my way of blowing off steam on my day off. I don't have to do it though if you would rather I can stay home."

"Don't be ridiculous. You have your routine and I'll eventually figure out mine."

I hated thinking of her being all alone.

"Why don't you guys come on over here?"

"No. I'll wait for them to get here first and then I'll drive over. Do you need anything?"

Did I need anything? I grinned from her even asking. No one ever did. Not that I minded. I loved hosting D&D nights, but it had always fallen on me. Even when others hosted, I was still the one that had to show up early and setup the game, put out the maps, and prepare everything. Sometimes that even meant bringing the food.

It meant the world to me that she had asked.

"I've got it, but thanks."

"Thanks for what?"

"For being you," I told her honestly.

"I'll see you as soon as Silas and Vada get here."

"Can't wait."

I meant it too. As much as I loved the game, I'd give it all up for time alone with my mate.

Pushing that thought from my head, I got started on the food.

Time flew by and soon there was a knock at the door as Tarron and Susan were the first to arrive.

"Hey, you came back!" I exclaimed, excited to see Susan return.

"Wouldn't miss it," she assured me. "Is Lucy here?"

"Soon. She's getting Vada settled over at her place."

"I guess next week we'll have the munchkin running around here, huh?" Tarron said.

I shrugged. "We'll see. I'm sure my parents will agree to watch her."

"So things didn't work out with Silas and Vada?" Susan asked.

"It was fine. They're babysitting again tonight."

"But by next week Lucy and little Vada will be officially living here. We move them this weekend, right?"

I grinned and nodded. I couldn't wait to have my girls home for good.

"That's great, Micah. So you've sealed your bond then?"

I groaned and rolled my eyes dramatically.

"I'm going to take that as a no," she said with a laugh.

"We've been a little busy," I tried to explain.

The door opened and others joined us as we were talking.

"I'll say," Christine added. "The whole Pack is talking about what Lucy did for Tabitha. It's like a miracle."

I smiled uneasily and nodded, not wanting to comment on it or try to explain that it wasn't just Lucy who had healed her.

I was worried about how people would react to such a powerful young witch if they found out the truth about Vada. For now, no one would suspect. Still, I knew we needed to tell Kyle and Kelsey. Perhaps Kelsey would even be willing to train her in the coming years.

Personally, I'd never seen or heard of a child so young demonstrating the level of power Vada had shown. I'd heard the stories of Kelsey and her sisters though and knew she had come into her powers at a very young age too. It made me wonder if these witches were actually born with their gifts and some were just more noticeable than others in the early years. Unfortunately, until recently I really hadn't had much experience with witches. Now they seemed to be everywhere.

I wasn't complaining. They didn't scare me. Quite the opposite actually. I was fascinated by them, even more so now that Lucy and Vada were in my life. I wanted to know everything about them and how to help them in whatever capacity they needed.

"Micah," Christine said sounding a little annoyed.

I looked up and sensed that she had probably tried more than once to get my attention.

"What?"

"Is Lucy coming? Everyone else is here."

"Yeah. She'll be here soon. You guys grab some food and settle in."

Lucy

Chapter 23

I hated running late, but by the time I went back through everything with Silas and Vada, time had simply slipped by me. Now I was debating whether I should even show up or not as I sat in front of Micah's house second guessing my plans to come.

A tap on my window startled me and I screamed.

Micah made a motion for me to roll down my window.

"Are you okay? You've been sitting out here for a few minutes already."

"How did you know that?"

He shrugged. "I just knew."

"Have you started the game yet?"

"No. We're waiting on you, so are you coming or not?"

I blushed, hating the thought of them holding their game up because of me. I honestly thought he would have already started by now.

"About time," Christine said snidely.

"Sorry," I muttered taking the open seat between her and Micah.

My leg bounced up and down as I tried to settle in. Without even looking my way, Micah started recounting the tales of our journey as a reminder of where we left off the week before. While he talked, his foot stretched out and wrapped around my leg.

The sudden contact with my mate calmed me instantly. I sighed and chanced a look at him. He just smirked and winked as he called the game into play.

My focus shifted as I allowed myself to be swept away into a magical world that had saved me time and time again.

Unfortunately, it went much too fast. I was sad to see Micah wrap things up and then having to say goodbye to new friends.

Susan and Tarron held back to help us clean up.

"You really don't have to," Micah insisted.

"No, it's cool. I know you aren't staying here at the moment," Tarron said.

"You aren't?" Susan asked.

"He's staying at my place until we arrange to move," I explained.

"Oh, that makes sense," she said with a smile as the four of us picked up and put food away.

"He already made arrangements for your move," Tarron blurted out.

"You did? When?"

Micah just shrugged. "You said this weekend, so I asked the guys if they'd pitch in and help out."

"Barring no unexpected mission popping up, I think you have all of Bravo unit coming to help Saturday. Silas insisted on it."

"Wow." I didn't know what to make of that. I'd never had friends I could just ask to help with something like that, let alone an entire team of them.

"It's okay," Susan said. "Took a little getting used to for me as well. Pack life around here is a new experience for me."

"I was raised in a Pack though. People still wouldn't just jump in to help like this," I blurted out.

"Well, in this Pack, that's normal. Please, everyone loves Doc and there are very few who wouldn't jump in to help him with anything, especially because he never abuses that," she insisted.

"Okay," I said feeling a bit overwhelmed, but grateful. "I'll see if his mom will watch Vada then."

"No need," Tarron said. "Emma, Vada, Susan, and Olivia will round up all the kids while we work."

"He's right. Emma and those of us that are pregnant tend to watch the kids and keep them out of the way. Shelby's crew will be there, and I think little Vada already knows them, right?"

I groaned. "Yeah. They're a bit of trouble together though. Four toddlers can apparently do quite a bit of damage together." I chuckled remembering how sick and miserable my poor baby was from her stay with the triplets.

"We'll make sure all the candy is out of reach," Tarron said with a laugh.

"I thought Ben said it was and that didn't stop them at all," Micah reminded him.

"Well, if you have a stash of concern around here, I can always put eyes on it with an alarm to go off if they get too close."

My jaw dropped, making Susan laugh.

"He means it too. My man loves his toys. Surveillance is his specialty on the team."

"Oh," I managed to say.

Bravo team had come to the rescue to shut down the Raglan facility I was held at. I'd seen them in action, but really wasn't sure I wanted to know what sort of other things they did for the Pack.

With the kitchen cleaned and the game put away, Susan and Tarron finally left.

She hugged me on their way out and whispered, "Let's get together soon, maybe next Wednesday while the boys play."

"I'd like that," I told her, surprised that I meant it.

Micah waved and shut the door behind me before turning and wrapping me up in his arms. His lips were on own mine catching my gasp of surprise. He was persistent and needy as I smiled against him, opening my lips in a sigh as his tongue sought mine.

I held onto his shoulders to steady myself. This man literally took my breath away.

He pulled back and gave me one more quick peck on the lips.

"I missed you today."

"Missed you, too," I confessed.

It was kind of pathetic just how much I'd missed him. Not that I wanted him to know that. I had no idea what to do with myself all day with no work, no toddler to entertain and chase after, and no Micah. Days off sucked.

Suddenly I was aware of just how alone we were as I looked down the hall to his bedroom. This could be it. We could seal our bond right here, right now.

But Micah pulled away. "Do you have everything?"

"Huh?"

"Let's get home and rescue our girl. How many texts of reassurance did Silas try to send tonight?"

"Uh, what?"

"Are you okay?" he asked with a frown.

"I'm fine." Embarrassed, I tried to shake off the lust throbbing through my body. Clearly Micah wasn't thinking about claiming me tonight.

"Vada, Luce. We need to go rescue Vada."

"Shit. Yeah, let's go."

Once in the car he turned to look at me.

"What were you thinking about back there instead?"

My cheeks burned and I turned my head to stare out the window refusing to answer his question.

"Nothing," I muttered.

"Damn. It must have been good. Next week we'll take Vada to Mom's and she can spend the night, and then you're going to tell me exactly what you were thinking for tonight."

I clamped my jaw and tried not to grin as I thought of all the things I'd really like to do with him.

Since the second Vada was born my entire focus and obsession has been on her. Tonight, I realized that had shifted to include Micah. I wasn't exactly sure when it had happened, but he was as much a part of my life now as she was.

That realization was a little terrifying. I counted on him. I trusted him. I'd never had anyone in my life that I could lean on like that before. Spending the day alone had really made me stop and realize that.

"Are you okay?" Micah asked.

I turned to look at him and grinned. "Never better."

Reaching for his hand, I linked our fingers together as he drove us home, just content to be there with him.

It felt empowering knowing this man was by my side. It was as if he somehow made all the darkness of my past a little lighter to bear. And for once, I was excited about what the future held.

He pulled up in front of the little house I was renting and put the car in park, but neither of us moved right away.

"I hope it was okay that I made arrangements for moving this weekend."

"What? Of course it's okay. We don't really have much, so it should go quickly. Most of the furniture and stuff here came with the house."

He shrugged. "I'm going to pick up some paint and stuff and have them clean out a room for Vada and paint it and everything, too. We'll need to babyproof."

My heart warmed at his concern for my daughter, no, our daughter.

Having him to share the burdens of raising an exceptional little witch with me made my eyes sting with tears. One escaped and slid down my cheek.

He reached over and swiped it away with his thumb.

"What is it?"

"Nothing, I promise. Happy tears. I never dreamed I'd find you. You don't know how lonely and scary life was before you came into it. I feel like I can finally breathe a little, like the weight of the world isn't entirely on my shoulders anymore."

He reached over and hugged me, kissing my forehead.

"I'll happily shoulder it all for the both of you, always. You'll never be alone again, Lucy."

"Thank you for loving me, and for loving my daughter."

"Our daughter," he corrected. "I wasn't joking about that."

"I know. Our daughter."

Before we got out of the car, Silas and Vada came running out of the house.

Micah's wolf went on full alert as he jumped from the car.

"What's wrong?" he demanded.

"Call just came in. Gotta run," Silas yelled over his shoulder. "Don't worry. She's still alive."

"She's fine," Vada assured me. "Already asleep and everything."

"Wow, I'm impressed."

"Come on," Silas barked.

Vada hugged me. "It was a lot easier this time. I just might survive these twins after all."

I smiled as I watched her jump into the car as they sped off.

"What would have happened if we hadn't just come home?" I wondered aloud.

"He would have left her here to watch our girl while he ran off to do his duty."

I considered that for a moment.

"I suppose it's not much different than us in that regard, huh? I mean you could get called out for an emergency at any second without notice, too."

"Yeah, I guess. I mean on call for anyone is like that in some regard I suppose."

As if we had just summoned fate, his phone rang.

Micah stared down at it with a frown. "Let's not talk about on call again anytime soon."

I laughed as he answered it.

"You want me to what? Yeah, okay. Fine. I'll be there in twenty. How long? Of course you don't know," he practically growled as he hung up the phone.

"What is it?"

"The mission Silas just got called out on, I've been summoned to go along."

"Does that happen often?"

"No, but it does happen."

"Will you be safe?"

"Yes, or as safe as possible at least. Don't worry. I'll be home before you know it."

I knew from talking to the other mates that there was no way he could know that for certain, but I appreciated the positivity while everything inside of me screamed not to let him go.

I'd had a front row seat to what Bravo team actually did and was well aware of the danger my mate could be walking into.

Pushing those fears aside, I hugged him tightly and then let him escort me into the house. He grabbed his bag he had taken to keeping at my place and then disappeared into Vada's room. I could hear him talking to her from where I sat on my bed trying not to freak out or cry. I needed to be strong for him.

"Hey sweet girl, I've got to leave for a bit, and I need you to watch after Mommy for me while I'm away. I promise you that nothing will keep me from coming back to you both. I know you can't hear me, and I don't want to wake you, but know I love you so much. See you soon."

Tears breached my eyelids and slowly slid down my cheeks.

This sweet man was mine. I felt my sharp canines start to form at the thought. It was long overdue to make that permanent. But now was not the time.

I swiped the tears away as he came back into the bedroom.

"It's up to you if you want to hold office hours tomorrow. I really don't know how long I'll be gone, but if I can't call and check in, one of the mates should contact you with an update. Sometimes they only get info out to one so they can spread the word."

"It's going to be fine," I told him, trying to summon up all the positivity I could muster. "We're going to be fine."

He pulled me into his embrace and kissed me.

"I hate leaving you."

"You told them twenty minutes. You have to go," I reminded him knowing this was the life I was signing on for and I had to be supportive no matter how much it was tearing me apart inside to watch him go.

"Yeah, I know."

He cradled my face with his hands and just stared at me like he was trying to memorize it and then he kissed me once more before grabbing his bag and turning to walk away.

"See you soon," he yelled back.

I sank back against my pillow and allowed myself time to cry. Then I dried it up and grew a backbone. This was my life, my perfectly imperfect life, and I was all in. If this is what that entailed, then so be it. I'd survived so much worse, and I'd survive this.

Micah

Chapter 24

Leaving Lucy hadn't been easy. In fact, it just might have been the hardest thing I'd ever had to do. I could see the tears streaking her cheeks. I knew she was worried. Hell, she of all people knew exactly the kind of work Bravo team did. I didn't know how to reassure her that it was going to be okay.

She'd put up a good face, but it still wasn't easy to leave her or Vada behind.

Because of that, I was grumpy and resented being called into duty when I reached the airfield and boarded the plane. They never told us where we were going or when we'd return. To me that was far worse than being on call for a medical emergency.

With everyone accounted for, the plane took off and only then did Silas pass out folders letting us know the details of the mission.

I scanned through the report and frowned.

"We're on a medical mission to help some vicuna in the Andes?"

"That would be correct," Silas confirmed.

"Why didn't you mention this before? Lucy could have helped a lot with this one."

"She has little Vada to watch out for," Silas pointed out.

"My parents would have watched her, or we could have brought her along to help too."

"Are you telling me Vada's a healer as well?"

I hesitated, regretting opening my big mouth, but it was too late for that, so I slowly nodded.

"Wow, you have two healers? That's crazy," Baine said.

I shrugged trying not to make a big deal out of it. There was no way we were going to keep Vada's gift a secret within the Pack. It might be the largest Pack in the world, but it was still like a small town filled with gossip. She was too young to fully control it and it was only a matter of time before others noticed.

"Is that how Lucy healed your grandmother?" Ben asked.

"Yeah. She was close on her own, but Vada gave her the power boost she needed to complete the healing," I confessed.

I knew I could trust these guys with anything, even this, but I didn't enjoy sharing my family's secrets like this. It was my job to protect Vada. Still, I wasn't an idiot. Having Bravo team in on this could only help down the road. They were the most elite special ops shifter team in the world, and they would protect my daughter against all outside threats if it ever came down to it.

"That's awesome. We could certainly use more healers in the Pack," Ben added.

I started to relax a little. For so many generations, witches were feared. They were forced into hiding and treated like dirty little secrets. Thanks to Kyle and Kelsey, those stereotypes were changing. We had welcomed many witches into our Pack and celebrated their individuality. Perhaps Vada wouldn't have to grow up in fear of her powers. Just maybe it could be a normal part of her life and nothing to be hidden or ashamed of.

I remembered how worried Lucy had been about me finding out she was a witch. I didn't want our daughter to ever go through that. She was perfect just the way she was, not an abomination or someone to be ashamed of, and I vowed to remind her of that every day of her life going forward.

She was unique and special. We would celebrate that and encourage her to just be herself. No hiding, just unashamedly Vada.

"So why haven't you sealed your bond with Lucy already?" Tarron blurted out.

I groaned. "I told you; we just haven't found the right time. It's going to happen though, soon."

The subject was thankfully changed as we chatted to pass the time. Before long, I dozed off and slept until the plane lurched to a stop waking me.

"Are we here?" I muttered, still sleepy.

"Yeah. Grab your gear and let's roll out. We have a hotel lined up here and will start the journey around noon. There's a team already on-site running lead for this. We're only here to assist as needed."

From what the report had said, the vicuna in the area were being poached. Their hides were being taken, leaving the poor animals to wither in pain until they died. It was brutal and unnecessary. There was absolutely no need for the hides when all they wanted was the wool.

These poachers were merciless and brutal. They were also idiots. By killing the vicuna instead of just shearing them, it was a one and done process. If they were smarter about it, they could harvest the wool each and every year, but there appeared to be more to it than just that. The hides were perceived as trophies for these poachers, and they truly didn't seem to care about the animals they left behind.

On the ground, we were met by none other than Jacob Winthrop himself. I was honestly surprised to see the man. He'd recently lost his wife in the final battle to defeat the Raglan and last I'd heard he was locked away in mourning.

"Jacob. I'm shocked to see you here," Silas confessed as the two men shook hands.

"When this call came in, I had to come see for myself. Such senseless brutality enrages me."

"Understandable from what we've been briefed on. Are you okay?"

"I'll never be okay again but locking myself up in a house filled with memories and drinking myself to death is not what Annie would have wanted for me."

Silas nodded.

None of us could even imagine what he was going through. By the time Lucy and I were together as long as he'd been with his wife, I would hope our bond would be fully sealed so I could peacefully follow her into death. As humans, Jacob had no such peace with the loss of his wife.

Jacob Winthrop was a prominent member of the Vendari, an ancient brotherhood dedicated to the survival and protection of shifters. I didn't know a lot about them, but despite their rogue offspring called the Raglan that was defeated by Bravo team, the Vendari were supposedly the good guys.

I struggled to trust any humans, but I knew many did.

"Clara and Gage are here with a team. They are already up the mountain working to try and save as many as possible," Jacob explained.

"Grant and Micah are happy to assist them."

"Wonderful. I have a car waiting to take them there now."

"I thought we were going to the hotel first," I protested, already feeling exhausted.

"The others will and catch up with us later. But we could really use the extra medical experience as quickly as possible. It's quite possibly one of the most gruesome scenes I've ever encountered, and timing is of the essence."

"Understood. We're ready to roll out," Grant said, speaking for the both of us.

I sighed. There was no point in protesting.

Jacob loaded us up into a Jeep and we immediately headed up the mountain while the rest of the team made their way to the hotel for a bit more sleep.

"I've asked them to track these poachers and stop this once and for all."

"How bad is it?" I asked.

"We have thirty-five animals fighting for their lives right now. And six very agitated and angry vicuna shifters ready to take action on their own. With the slow extinction of the vicunas, they've been working on repopulating the area. So, as you can imagine, this is very personal to them. These were their children and the dedication and sacrifice of years of work."

"What do we know about the vicuna?" Grant asked. "I don't think I've ever even heard of such a thing."

"They are closely related to the alpaca, a little smaller in size, but similar in appearance. They are a shy, docile creature who once roamed these mountains in great herds. Thanks to deforestation and poachers, amongst other things, their numbers have been drastically declining. Repopulating them is no small feat. Like their domesticated cousins, they can only conceive once a year with a long gestational period, resulting in only one offspring a year. The six shifters here are on a rotation for reproduction. There are three mated couples, and they are taking turns so that two of the females are pregnant each year giving them one of every three years off."

"I can't even imagine that kind of sacrifice," I confessed.

"Yes, and with only two new additions to the herds each year, they can't afford to lose a single one."

"What about the wild animals? Are they not producing?" Grant asked.

"Good question. They are, which has been helping quite a bit as of late. There was talk of the shifters moving to only one new addition a year, and now this."

I could hear the heaviness in his words. I had no idea what I was walking into, but whatever it was, it was bad.

Using my bag as a makeshift pillow, I closed my eyes and forced myself to go to sleep while Jacob and Grant chatted some more. I'd heard enough and unlike Bravo team, I wasn't exactly used to these spontaneous calls resulting in little sleep. The most I had to deal with was a rare crisis or the occasional late-night birth. Yes, I was on call twenty-four seven, three-hundred and sixty-five days a year, but I could count on one hand just how many middle of the night calls came in as a result of that.

I wasn't certain how long I had slept, but it felt like I'd just closed my eyes when the Jeep came to a stop.

"We're here," Grant informed me.

Groggily, I forced myself to sit up and look out. The area was beautiful, and it was hard to believe there was even a human within miles of the place. A large white tent was set in a field as a team pulled up with a flatbed truck unloading the bodies of the vicuna. I couldn't tell from here if they were alive or dead.

Grant took off at a sprint to assist. Without even thinking, I chased after him. The closer we got the louder the screams and cries could be heard.

I couldn't ever remember losing my stomach on a job before, but if it was going to happen, it would be here and now.

Bloodied bodies were unloaded as teams carried them into the field tent where a makeshift medical center had been established.

"Come on. I'm going to put you with our team out of Collier."

I sniffed the air, trying to move past the smell of blood and decay.

"Humans?" I whispered.

He nodded. "Verndari. You're safe here. I pulled in every resource I have for this."

I followed behind him in silence, just taking it all in until I saw a familiar face.

"Clara!"

She paused from talking to a group of people and turned my way. Her weary face lit up when she saw me.

"Micah? Wow, you really did pull in every resource possible," she said admiringly to Jacob.

"No expense spared for this. We're doing everything we can to help. Excuse me."

We both watched him leave.

"Is he okay?" I asked her.

She shrugged. "I don't know. I feel like he's trying to pay penance or something."

"He should be mourning the loss of his wife still."

Clara sighed. "Everyone mourns differently. Before this he was locked in his house refusing to see anyone, so maybe having a job to do is helping him in some weird way. Don't worry. We're all keeping an eye on him."

"Hey Gage," I said, shaking the man's hand as Clara's mate approached us.

"Micah? Man, they'll take anyone for this mission, huh?" he teased. "It's great to see you."

"You guys as well. It's been a while. But I'm not really here to socialize. So put me to work."

Clara snorted. "So anxious. This one isn't easy."

"I've heard. And I wish they had briefed me before we left. I would have insisted on bringing my mate along."

I scowled in frustration. Part of me was glad Lucy wasn't here to see all of this, but there was also a big part of me that understood how much good she could have done here.

"Your mate? I hadn't heard you'd taken one."

Groaning, I rolled my eyes. "Not officially yet. We're trying, but life keeps getting in the way."

"Is she a doctor as well?"

"Healer," I explained.

Clara groaned this time. "We definitely could have used her here."

"I know. But you got me instead, so point me in a direction and put me to work."

She did. The rest of my day was spent applying salves and trying to stop the bleeding on as many of the creatures as possible.

They were in so much pain and I knew their cries would haunt me for a very long time.

After a while, I became immune to the stench of the place and popped in my headphones to crank up some music as loud as possible. It didn't drown out all the noise, but enough to let me think straight.

The work was endless and tiring. Day turned to night, night into day, and still we pressed on until every last possible vicuna that could be saved was. Of the initial thirty-five we were able to stabilize twenty-two of them. Another dozen had come in as well, but it was too late for most of them, only four additional survived.

"Hey, take a break and get some sleep," Gage finally told me.

I shook my head. "There's still work to be done."

"And you won't be able to help them without nourishment and sleep. Everyone else has taken their turn. You're the last man standing as it is, so please, go and sleep."

I didn't tell him that I didn't think I could. I wasn't trained in trauma such as this and I knew that when I closed my eyes, I'd still see them. I'd still hear them. I didn't know how to just turn that off.

He was persistent though until I finally caved and walked away. My entire body was exhausted, but I forced myself to eat something before laying down on one of the cots in the corner.

Certain I wasn't going to sleep, I cranked up my music once more and just closed my eyes allowing my body to at least rest.

Much to my surprise, some time later, Clara woke me up. I jumped, unaware that I had even fallen asleep.

"Westin Force is back."

I nodded wiping my eyes and trying to get my bearings straight.

Gage grinned down on me. "That's what happens when you push it too long. You'll learn."

I smiled but couldn't help thinking that I hoped I never learned. This wasn't the sort of work I wanted to do all the time. I was happy to pitch in and help when needed, but if I did this all the time, it would kill me. I didn't know how to let it go and just walk away.

Yet, with the vicuna we could save now stable, I did just that. Grant seemed to understand more than the others because he had been there for it all. He helped me a lot to process all that happened on the way home.

The others were quiet and seemed to be dealing with their own crap. I'd been told the poachers had been hunted down and handled. I didn't ask what that meant, but from the looks of my friends' faces, I could guess.

I shuddered thinking of how they did these sort of missions all the time. Sometimes they were called away two or three times a week and others for weeks at a time. Was it always this hard?

I didn't think I wanted to know. I just wanted to get home to my mate and our daughter, back to the safe life we had there where poachers weren't a concern.

Lucy, I thought with a smile. She was my home now and I couldn't wait to get back and make it official. I looked down at my watch noting the date.

Days had blurred together, and I didn't realize it was already Saturday.

Lucy and Vada were supposed to be moving in with me today. I'd had it all planned out and now I didn't see how we could make it happen. There was no way I could ask these guys to come over after all we'd just been through.

Looking out the window I tried not to let it discourage me. So what if it wasn't going to be perfect? I'd get us there and I could always move over their stuff at least. Maybe tomorrow. I wasn't sure I was going to do anything more than crash today when I got home.

Lucy

Chapter 25

It was crazy how much I missed Micah. He hadn't been gone even twenty-four hours and I felt lost without him. How had this happened?

Vada was incessantly asking about him too, which wasn't helping me any. She missed him as much as I did and didn't understand why he wasn't there when she awoke the next morning. Because of that I decided that it was imperative that we stick to our usual routine. So, I had gotten up and gotten her ready for school. We'd had breakfast together before I dropped her off and then drove to the clinic.

I didn't have to open the office today. Word spread quickly throughout the Pack, and I was certain no one was expecting it, but I needed something to do even if it was just paperwork. Anything to keep my mind preoccupied.

Not ten minutes after I flipped the sign over to open, the bell over the front door had jingled.

I sighed, trying not to be frustrated. I hadn't even finished my morning cup of coffee.

"This was your decision, Lucy," I reminded myself aloud.

Taking a deep breath and planting a smile on my face, I walked to the front desk and then fought not to roll my eyes.

"Hello, Nonna."

"Good morning, Lucy. She's here!" she yelled out the door.

Soon two other women walked in.

"Tabitha? Is everything okay?" I asked, surprised to see Micah's grandmother there.

"Never better, Lucy."

"If I ever start to lose my mind, I'm coming to you," the other woman said.

"Birdie!" Tabitha scolded. "That's a terrible thing to say."

"You know what I mean. I'm too old for false pretenses and that politically correct nonsense."

"We heard Micah was called out of town with Bravo company," Nonna said. "I have it on good authority."

"I'm sure you do," I said with a smile, knowing her favorite adopted grandson was a prominent member of the team.

"Have you heard from him yet?"

"They haven't even been gone twenty-four hours yet. So no. Have you heard from Tarron?"

She sighed. "No. I always worry when he's away. Gives me panic attacks or something."

"You mean gossip attacks, right?" Birdie said.

Her snowy white hair and sharp blue eyes were mesmerizing. Something about her made it feel as if she were an old soul who had seen much in her life, but there was a spark of mischief in her eyes that made her seem far younger.

"Don't you pay her no mind," she told me. "She just likes to fish for information. That's all. Kills her when he's away and she doesn't have the latest and greatest of Force gossip at her disposal."

"I can't wait to meet her Tarron. He sure sounds like quite the character," Tabitha added.

"Was there something I can do for you ladies this morning?" I finally asked, curious as to why they were even here.

"Not at all. We just wanted to stop by and check on you," she explained.

"That's right. Altruistic and all. I wasn't fishing or anything," Nonna insisted, but even I knew better despite the fact that the other two women started laughing. "I mean it. How are you holding up, Lucy?"

I smiled. "I'm fine. Thank you for asking."

"Well, we brought you some coffee," Tabitha said holding out an extra cup.

Nonna looked around and then spotted a table in the corner. She cleared it off and dragged it over to the center of the waiting room while Birdie gathered four chairs then pulled a tablecloth from her purse and covered the small table.

Next, Nonna pulled out a small flower arrangement from her bag along with four small plates and silverware.

Tabitha gave me a sheepish look before she took out a Tupperware container of muffins and another of fresh fruit.

Before I knew what was happening, we had a full tea party of sorts in the middle of the waiting room.

I shook my head.

"You guys had all of this in your purses?"

Micah's grandmother gave me a sly smile.

"A lady is always prepared for anything life throws her way."

"Oh, is that right?" I teased with a laugh.

They chatted the morning away having my side in stitches from laughing at their stories. I learned that Birdie was the matriarch of Westin Pack at one hundred and twenty-six years old. I could hardly believe it when she confessed it. She looked amazing, and while I knew that wolf shifters tended to look younger, be healthier, and even live longer than humans, I'd never met someone that old before.

There were so many external factors that often led to our kind dying prematurely, especially in today's world. I was fascinated just talking with her and hearing the stories of her life and how things had changed. Her parents had been first generation born in San Marco. I was in awe just listening to her speak.

"Well, you are certainly an amazing lady, Ms. Birdie."

"Nothing amazing about me. Just a lot of stories from a long life lived."

The three women stayed and chatted, just keeping me company until Marshall showed up with a scowl on his face.

"This is where you've been hiding all day?" he said gruffly.

"Well, I had to check on my guardian angel and make sure she's okay while Micah's out of town."

He shook his head. "It's time for lunch. Are you ditching me for that too?"

The three women laughed but Tabitha rose, said goodbye, and left with him.

"He's one of the good ones," Birdie said. "Your Micah is too."

I smiled. I already knew that. I was lucky to have such an amazing man by my side.

"We should head out, too. You don't need to stick around this place all day. Everyone knows Micah's out of town," Nonna assured me.

"Thanks, but I have some paperwork and stuff I'd like to get sorted out just the same. Helps to stay busy."

"You call if you need anything at all," Nonna told me.

Tears pricked my eyes as I tried to pull it together long enough for them to leave. It had been a long time since anyone cared enough about me to say such a thing. If I were being honest, I wasn't sure anyone in my life had ever cared that much, at least not until I moved to San Marco.

I was still pondering that when the bell over the door sounded again.

"Be right there," I yelled out.

"Take your time," a familiar voice hollered back.

I froze and then slowly walked back to the front only to find Shelby, Susan, Vada, Emma, Olivia, and Alaina were standing around the lobby talking.

"What are you guys doing here?"

"Just checking on you. We all know how hard it can be when the guys are away," Shelby said.

"Especially your first time," Alaina added.

"We take care of each other," Emma explained.

"And now, you're one of us," Susan said with a smile.

"Thanks, but this wasn't necessary. Really. I'm fine."

"We all say that." Olivia rolled her eyes. "Put on a good front, and all that. But we don't do that with each other. That's for outsiders."

"We're family and we have to stick together." Vada smiled at me.

Of everyone here, she was the one who knew how desperately I needed and wanted to hear that.

"And we're taking the day off," Alaina said. "So close up the clinic, and let's go."

"Go? Where?"

"Down to the lake. It's too pretty of a day to be cooped up with our worry."

"Oh, um, I guess that's okay."

"No one is coming. They all know Micah left with Bravo and despite the rumors of what you did for his grandmother, it would have to be pretty bad or simple curiosity for someone to come in knowing he's away."

I sighed knowing they were right.

"I know," I conceded. "But it seemed like a good way to pass the time."

"Not today," Susan said.

"Yup, today, we pass the time together. It helps a ton. Trust us," Olivia insisted.

"Okay," I said, caving quickly because being alone with my worries wasn't going to pass the time very quickly. It was only going to drive me insane.

I grabbed my purse and ushered them out so I could lock up.

The rest of the day went by quickly, relaxing by the lake and laughing with the girls. It was one of the most therapeutic days I'd ever experienced. My stomach hurt from laughing so much.

As the afternoon passed by and it was time to get Vada from school, I begrudgingly said goodbye.

"Don't go," Susan protested.

"I have to pick up my daughter. You guys will understand soon." Nearly half of them were pregnant after all.

"Call Lorraine and have her pick her up. She'll be happy to," Olivia insisted.

"Yes. We're too busy having a mental health day," Emma added.

"I can't do that. It's too last minute."

"Do it!" Vada ordered.

I sighed, feeling pressured to obey.

"Fine. I'll see." I pulled out my phone and dialed Lorraine's number.

"Hello? Lucy? Is everything okay?"

"Everything's fine. I didn't mean to scare you."

"No, of course not. What can I do for you?"

"Um, I really hate to ask this, but are you busy right now?"

"Not really, just starting to think of dinner. Would you and Vada like to join us?" she asked. I could hear the hope in her voice.

"Actually, I was wondering if maybe you would have time to pick Vada up from school today?"

"Really? You mean it?"

"I mean, if it's a problem, it's fine. I've just been kidnapped by the Bravo team mates and they are reluctant to let me go."

"That's fantastic, Lucy! Stay. Enjoy yourself. They're a great bunch of ladies, especially right now with Micah gone. I'm happy to hear they are including you. Don't worry about a thing. I'm happy to pick up my sweet grandpup. Thrilled even. I'll make sure she gets fed and you can pick her up whenever you like, or if you need a night to yourself, she's always welcome to spend the night."

"I'm not sure I'm quite ready for that," I admitted. "But I'm getting there."

"Baby steps. This is a good start," she told me. "Enjoy your time off. I promise you Vada is in excellent hands."

"Thanks, Lorraine."

As soon as I hung up, I called Vanessa and let her know that Vada's grandmother was going to be picking her up.

It was strange to rely on others, but it also felt right.

When I turned back to the others, they were all watching me. They started to cheer as Olivia got up and hugged me.

"I'm proud of you for agreeing to that. It wasn't easy for me to rely on anyone when it was just me and Macie, well, except my brothers. I guess we all need family in our lives, huh?"

"More than I realized," I confessed.

We talked and laughed late into the night. I felt horrible about the late hour as I pulled up to Lorraine and Mallick's house.

The light was still on, and the door opened before I even knocked on the door.

"She's sleeping soundly. We played hard and wore her out," Mallick said proudly.

"Is that Lucy?" Lorraine asked, joining us in the hallway.

"I'm really sorry it's so late."

"Don't be," she insisted, cutting off my apology. "We're just grateful that you trusted us to care for her tonight. You have no idea how much that meant to the both of us. I know this isn't easy on you, and we've learned enough to understand why, but we couldn't possibly love that girl more if she was our own flesh and blood."

"Pretty sure she'd fight anyone who tried to argue that's not our granddaughter," Mallick teased.

"Damn straight I would," Lorraine cursed.

I followed them back to the playroom they had set up for Vada, complete with a bed fit for a princess. She was sound asleep.

I leaned down and kissed her sweet head. She smelled freshly bathed and I didn't recognize the pajamas she wore, but I didn't question it.

"You know, we do have a guest room and you're welcome to stay if you'd rather not wake her," Lorraine said. That optimistic tone was back in her voice.

"Are you sure?" I asked. I was too tired to argue it and honestly my bed felt empty without Micah in it. Perhaps a change of scenery would help.

"The bathroom connects the two rooms, so you can leave the doors open in case she wakes in the night."

Mallick rolled his eyes and handed me a nursery camera.

"Or you can just keep this, and you'll hear her when she wakes. We wanted to make sure we could get to her quickly so she wouldn't get too scared in a new place."

Again, I was blown away by how thoughtful they both were.

"Thank you," I said, surprising us all when I hugged Lorraine and then Mallick. "It's funny. It's just been me and Vada for so long, and now the house feels so empty without Micah."

They nodded in understanding.

"We'll leave you be. Get a good night's sleep. I'll make breakfast in the morning," she said before dragging her mate out of the nursery before I could protest.

I just smiled, grateful for the both of them.

I checked on Vada one last time and then headed to the room next door, climbed into bed, and fell fast asleep.

*****

Vada slept through the night, and miraculously, I did too. True to her word, Lorraine had breakfast ready. I thought I was going to have to swing by the house to get her dressed for school, but I supposed I shouldn't have been surprised when I discovered a whole closet full of clothes for Vada.

Shaking my head, I let her pick out an outfit and helped her dress for the day before we followed our noses to the kitchen.

"Lorraine, you didn't have to make a feast for us."

"Nonsense. A growing pup needs a good strong breakfast to start the day."

I laughed and just shook my head.

We both ate our fill before thanking them again for the thousandth time as I rushed out of the door to get Vada to school.

Afterwards, I contemplated my options and decided the others were right. No one was going to be seeking medical treatment knowing Micah was out of town. Plus, it was Friday and I was supposed to be moving the next day.

I had no way of knowing if Micah would be back in time, but I wanted to be ready just in case, so I drove home, changed into comfy clothes, and got to work packing.

Shortly before lunch, Lorraine called to see what I was up to and invite me to lunch.

I looked down at my watch, surprised to see the time.

"Wow, I didn't even realize the morning had snuck by me. I'm just here packing."

"Packing?"

"Yeah, I know it's a little silly. I don't even know when Micah will be home, but we were supposed to move out of my rental and into his house this weekend."

"You were?"

"Yes. So, I figured I could at least start packing and clean things up here just in case. I want to be ready."

It sounded silly to say it out loud.

"Well, do you need some help? I could bring sandwiches over. You do have to eat."

There was that hope tinged in her voice once more. It wasn't like me to accept help easily, but I found myself agreeing.

When I got off the phone with her, it rang again almost immediately.

"Hello?"

"Hey Lucy, just wanted to check in on you," Susan said.

"I'm fine. Lorraine's bringing lunch over. I'm just packing."

"Packing? What? Why?" she asked in a panic.

"Relax. Vada and I were supposed to move to Micah's tomorrow. I know they probably won't be home in time to do it this weekend now, but I figured I could start getting ready at least."

"Oh, right. I forgot about that. Tarron actually left me the list of everything Micah wanted done tomorrow. We haven't heard from Bravo yet. That's not really uncommon for a spontaneous mission like this, but Delta's in town. I'll make some calls and see if the guys are willing to pitch in. Maybe we can get you two moved this weekend after all."

"Really? Wait, he left a list? I told him we didn't have much, a couple carloads maybe. I could probably have Lorraine watch Vada and do it myself even."

"Oh girl, there's a lot more to it than that." She laughed. "Don't worry about a thing. I'm on it. Do you have a key to his house?"

My heart sunk. "No, I don't. So much for that idea."

"Well don't give up yet. Delta can always find a way in if they have to, but I bet his parents have a key for emergencies. Ask her when she gets there."

"Yeah, okay. I'll do that."

"And do you need some help? Shelby and Emma are back to their normal routine today, but the rest of us can come and help."

"Honestly I don't think there's enough to do to bother, but if you guys just want to come and see for yourself, you're welcome to."

"I'll grab some lunch and make some calls. I don't know who's available, but I'll swing by this afternoon and help where I can."

Everything seemed to move at warp speed from there. Lorraine showed up with lunch. Turned out she did have a spare key to Micah's after all. She stuck around to help as Susan and Alaina came by to get me packed. They'd made all the arrangements for move day, too.

It felt weird to be proceeding without Micah. But Saturday came quickly, and things were rolling with or without my consent.

"Susan, what if he changed his mind? I'm not sure this is such a good idea."

She laughed. "Trust me. That boy is never going to change his mind when it comes to choosing you."

I blushed at her words. I hoped she was right. We hadn't exactly sealed our bond or made it official yet.

That didn't seem to matter to anyone but me.

Lorraine and Mallick were babysitting Vada at their house despite the offer by the others. She'd practically insisted on it and I had to admit that knowing she was with them eased a bit of my anxiety.

By the time I got to Micah's house, it felt like a construction zone. Men I had never seen before were moving furniture, cleaning rooms, painting, it was insane.

"What is going on?" I squeaked out.

Susan just laughed. "I told you he left a list. This is what Micah wanted."

"Who are all these people and where did they come from?"

"This is Westin Force Delta team. They rarely go out into the field. Their role is more like Pack security. Michael, this is Lucy."

"Hi," he said, barely stopping long enough to nod my way before he was off barking orders to someone.

"He's the team lead. Over there you have Tucker, Linc, and Walker. I think Colin and Lachlan are painting back in what will soon be Vada's room," she explained.

"Micah really left instructions for all of this?"

"Well, he gave Tarron the instructions for all he wanted done this weekend and Tarron left the list with me in case they didn't get back in time."

"And you really think Micah would be okay with all of this?"

"Oh, hell no. He'd likely freak out if he knew Delta was here, which is why we aren't going to leave you alone for even a second. If I have to go somewhere, someone else will come to relieve me."

"What's wrong with Delta? Why does he have a problem with them?"

"Girl, he has not yet claimed you, and all but one of these sexy Delta men are unmated."

"Oh," I said as I started to understand.

"But he'll be grateful it's all done. So don't worry about a thing."

The guys worked tirelessly while Susan rounded up a few more volunteers to assist us with moving our things over. In truth I had a lot more than I expected. It was amazing how quickly things seemed to have accumulated, but after a few caravans back and forth, we had everything in, piled up in the living room, and began sorting based on rooms.

I was happy to see that taking my time and marking each of the boxes had paid off. It made it so much easier to know what belonged in the kitchen verses the bedroom and so on.

"This bedroom is all painted," a guy yelled down the hall in a deep Australian accent.

"Thanks Lachlan," Susan yelled back.

The man that approached was as sexy as the voice. I felt absolutely nothing towards him, but I could appreciate a fine looking man when I saw one.

"We have fans going and the window open, but I'm not sure we'll be able to move things in until tomorrow. It needs to dry."

I was a little disappointed to hear it, but I knew we could stay at Micah's parents' house again if we needed to.

"Great. In that case, you guys can take a break and then help sort the rest of these boxes into the right rooms."

"Where did those other three guy go?" I asked, realizing I hadn't seen them in a while.

"They're out back building the swing set," Lachlan told me.

"The what?"

"It's on the list," Susan insisted.

"What else is on this list?" I asked, snatching the paper from Susan's hand.

Lachlan stood right behind me as he peered over my shoulder to read it for himself. But when he leaned in to point something out, a low growl halted us all.

I looked up to see a wild-eyed Micah standing in the doorway. His eyes were fixed on Lachlan as he growled again.

Bravo team was right behind him. The first thing I noticed was how exhausted they all looked. I knew, without being told, that it must have been a long, hard mission for all of them.

"Well, go calm him down already," Susan insisted giving me a little shove that earned her a growl too.

She didn't have to tell me twice as I ran to my mate and wrapped my arms around his neck.

"What is all of this about?" Tarron asked his mate.

"We weren't sure you guys would get back in time, so I had to improvise."

"With an entire team of unmated males?"

Micah shook at the thought as he looked around. His eyes were still wild.

"Come on, let me show you what they've done," I said, trying hard not to make a big deal out of it.

I took his hand, and we walked down the hall, stopping at Vada's room. Delta team had all retreated outside to assist with the playset, but I knew their scent was still everywhere and it was driving Micah insane.

After inspecting the freshly painted room, he grabbed my hand and pulled me towards the bedroom.

"Micah, we have a house full of people," I warned him.

He responded by grunting and then throwing me over his shoulder and carrying me to his room. He then strolled right into the giant walk-in closet and kicked the door shut before setting me down and pressing my back up against the door.

I was pinned. Trapped. It should have been freaking me out, but instead, it was kind of a turn on.

His wolf was close to the surface. I could feel him.

"Mine," he growled as he nuzzled my neck, and his hands frantically tore off my clothes.

"Micah," I squeaked out in surprise.

His hands were everywhere lighting my body up like it was on fire.

I reached down and undid his pants pushing them to the ground along with his underwear.

It was insane. There were at least a dozen people in the house and here wc were in the closet about to go at it like rabbits.

"Mine," he growled again and this time I felt the sharp prick of his teeth on my neck while at the same time he thrusted inside me.

I gasped, and then moaned as my canines elongated.

Finally, I thought as I bit into his neck.

It was crazy, yet long overdue. And in that moment, everything and everyone else faded away. It was as if Micah and I were the only two people left in the world.

Connected as one, a frenzy took hold as he pounded into me, and my back banged against the closet door. I couldn't get close enough to him as my legs tightened around his waist. I wanted him deeper inside of me. The taste of his blood fresh in my mouth. It was as if I were completely uninhibited.

My nails scratched down his back. He moaned against my neck caught up in his own needs.

Our bodies moved in perfect sync. I never dreamed it would be like this.

His thrusts became faster, harder, more sporadic as I felt my own desires heighten. I pulled back from his neck breaking our connection as I gasped for air.

"Yes," I cried out, needing him with a desperation I didn't know was possible.

As I reached my peak, my entire body tightened. I found his lips, unsure of when he'd pulled away from my neck, as I kissed him with all the love and desire I felt for him.

"Mine," he growled causing my entire body to shudder.

"Mine," I growled back at him rocking my body into his one last time as he found his release and let go.

Breathless and shaky, I clung to him.

We stood there like that, pressed against the closet door as I tried to regain some sense of composure. Never had I imagined our mating quite like that, but I wouldn't change it for anything.

Micah finally leaned back to look at me. He gave me a big grin.

"Missed you," he said, with a quick peck to my lips.

I laughed. "Missed you, too."

"Are you okay?"

I smiled reassuringly. "Never better."

It suddenly dawned on me that the house around us was quiet.

"Is there a dampener in here?" I asked.

"No, why?"

"It's just oddly quiet."

We redressed and hand-in-hand walked back out to the living room. There was no one in the house. I heard them nearby though and tugged Micah along as we walked to the backyard where everyone was hanging out.

"What's going on?" I asked Susan.

Tarron just laughed.

"Next time you want some alone time, just say so. You didn't have to scent up the entire house to make your point."

Micah groaned.

"You didn't!"

"There was an entire special forces team of unmated males in my house. What did you expect?"

"Did you at least seal the deal?" Silas yelled out.

Everyone was watching us as my mouth fell open and my cheeks burned.

Cheers went up all around as Micah responded.

"Hell yeah, I did! This one's mine forever."

Micah

Epilogue

"Time to wake up, birthday girl," I whispered.

Vada groaned and stretched. She was sleeping well these days. The nightmares subsided for the time being.

We were all settled into the house and into our new routine. I loved waking up every morning with Lucy in my arms, but then I would leave her to sleep as I awoke our daughter for some quiet time with her each day.

Today was a big day and I couldn't wait to start it.

"Birfday? It my birfday, Doc?"

"Yes, big girl. You're officially three today."

She gasped and then clapped, going from groggy to wide awake in about two point six seconds.

I swooped her up into my arms and swung her around the room.

"Wow, you are a big girl now."

She giggled.

"Want to help me make some special birthday pancakes?"

"Yes, pease."

Maybe it was selfish of me, and I should have made her a special breakfast before I woke her up, but I couldn't help it. I loved our morning time together and especially on this day wanted to share that with her.

I set her down on the counter and pulled out a bowl and spoon. I poured in the ingredients for pancakes while she stirred for me. No, they weren't perfect. Sometimes they were a little lumpy, but it was okay, because we made them together.

She sat there watching and giggling as we chatted, and I flipped pancakes in the hot skillet.

I loved being her dad and I couldn't believe my baby girl was three years old already.

"So, what do you want for your birthday today?" I asked her.

"A baby brudder," she proudly announced.

I nearly choked. "What?"

"A baby brudder. I gonna be a big sister."

I smiled. "Maybe someday. But what do you want today for your birthday?"

She huffed and asked to get down. I lifted her off the counter and set her on the floor before turning back to the pancakes.

Vada ran down the hallway.

"Don't wake Mommy yet," I whisper yelled after her.

Vada returned a little while later dressed in jeans in a pink T-shirt that read 'Big Sister'.

She grinned up at me and handed me a gift bag.

I squatted down to her level.

"Where did you get that shirt?"

"Open it," she said instead of answering.

"Sweetie, today's your birthday. Presents are for you, not me."

"Open it," she insisted.

Slowly I did, first pulling out an envelope.

Vada's face lit up as she nodded.

I opened it and read the letter inside.

My breath caught in my chest.

"Vada? Where did you get this?"

She giggled. "It says you're my daddy now."

She threw her little arms around my neck and kissed my cheek as I fought back tears.

I hugged her tightly, but it only lasted a few seconds before she wiggled away, grabbed the bag to pull out a positive pregnancy test followed by a baby onsie that read 'I have the Best Dad in the World'.

I struggled to breathe. *Could this be real?*

I snatched Vada up in my arms and took the bag and items with me to the bedroom.

"Lucy. Wake up."

"What's wrong?" she asked in a sleepy voice.

"Surprise!" Vada yelled.

Lucy groaned seeing the shirt she was wearing and no doubt the look of confusion on my face. When she spotted the bag in my hand, she frowned then turned and tickled Vada.

"You little munchkin. We agreed to do that together tonight."

Vada squealed with happiness.

"So, it's all real? You're pregnant?"

"Vada has everything for her birfday," our now three-year-old announced. "Mommy. Daddy," she said pointing to me before laying her head on Lucy's belly. "And baby brudder."

Lucy scowled at her. "I told you, we don't know for sure it's a brother. It could be a sister."

"No. Brudder," she insisted.

I just stared at them both in awe.

"Surprise," Lucy finally said in a weak voice. "I'm sorry. This isn't how I planned it at all."

"But you are pregnant?"

"I am."

"And the adoption papers are finalized, legal, and binding?"

"They are."

"I love you," I told her, leaning down to kiss my mate as our daughter squealed in disgusted delight, trying to wedge herself between us.

I'd never truly imagined what family life would look like, but this seemed pretty damned perfect to me.

*****

I hope you enjoyed Micah and Lucy's story!

Be sure to check out more in the Westin Pack series starting with Kyle and Kelsey's story in One True Mate.

Want more of the Westin Force team?
If so, you can read their stories in my Westin Force series.
Grant and Taylor are up first in Fierce Impact.

Dear Reader,

Thanks for reading Healing Fate. If you enjoyed Micah & Lucy's story, please consider dropping a review. https://mybook.to/Westin7 It helps more than you know.

For further information on my books, events, and life in general, I can be found online here:

Website: www.julietrettel.com

www.facebook.com/authorjulietrettel

www.instragram.com/julie.trettel

https://www.bookbub.com/authors/julie-trettel

http://www.goodreads.com/author/show/14703924.Julie_Trettel

http://www.amazon.com/Julie_Trettel/e/B018HS9GXS

Sign up for my Newsletter with a free Westin Pack Short Story!
https://dl.bookfunnel.com/add9nm91rs

Love my books?
Join my Reader Group, Julie Trettel's Book Lover's on Facebook!
https://www.facebook.com/groups/compounderspod7

With love and thanks,
Julie Trettel

More books by Julie Trettel!

Westin Pack
One True Mate
Fighting Destiny
Forever Mine
Confusing Hearts
Can't Be Love
Under a Harvest Moon

Collier Pack
Breathe Again
Run Free
In Plain Sight
Broken Chains
Coming Home
Holiday Surprise

ARC Shifters
Pack's Promise
Winter's Promise
Midnight Promise
iPromise
New Promise
Don't Promise
Forgotten Promise
Hidden Promise
All-Star Promise

Westin Force
Fierce Impact
Rising Storm
Collision Course
Technical Threat
Final Extraction
Waging War

Six Pack Shifters
His Destined Mate
His True Mate
His Chosen Mate

Westin Force Delta
High Risk
Nothing to Chance

Bonus Westin World Books
Ravenden
A Collier First Christmas
Shifter Marked and Claimed
Panther's Pride: The Shifter Trials
Christmas at Kaitlyn's Place

More books by: Jules Trettel!

Armstrong Academy
Louis and the Secrets of the Ring
Octavia and the Tiny Tornadoes
William and the Look Alike
Hannah and the Sea of Tears
Eamon and the Mysteries of Magic
May and the Strawberry Scented Catastrophe
Gil and the Hidden Tunnels
Elaina and the History of Helios
Alaric and the Shaky Start
Mack and the Disappearing Act
Halloween and the Secret's Blown
Ivan and the Masked Crusader
Dani and the Frozen Mishaps

Stones of Amaria
Legends of Sorcery
Ruins of Magic
Keeper of Light
Fall of Darkness

The Compounders Series
The Compounders: Book1
Dissension
Discontent
Sedition

About the Author

Julie Trettel is a USA Today Bestselling Author of Paranormal Romance. She comes from a long line of story tellers. Writing has always been a stress reliever and escape for her to manage the crazy demands of juggling time and schedules between work and an active family of six. In her "free time," she enjoys traveling, reading, outdoor activities, and spending time with family and friends.

Visit

www.JulieTrettel.com

Made in the USA
Monee, IL
26 May 2023

34691694R00127